FLUX DRIVES DID NOT FAIL ...

At sixty thousand feet the *Dancer's* hydrogen-powered flux drive simply quit. The ship was not yet at escape velocity, and as the thrusters lost power, alarms began to clang.

Aaron had only seconds before the ship's upward momentum failed. The restart procedures, one, two, three, failed. Space ships carried no escape pods, no parachutes. Aaron had one option left. He could fire the Blink Generator. But firing a Blink Generator within a planet's atmosphere might create widespread devastation. That was his only choice, risk an innocent world's safety—or die himself. Death or devastation—Aaron had to decide now!

THE DARK SIDE

Zach Hughes

A SIGNET BOOK

NEW AMERICAN LIBRARY

Copyright © 1987 by Hugh Zachary

SIGNET TRADEMARK REG. U.S. PAT. OFF. AND FOREIGN COUNTRIES
REGISTERED TRADEMARK—MARCA REGISTRADA
HECHO EN CHICAGO, U.S.A.

SIGNET, SIGNET CLASSIC, MENTOR, ONYX, PLUME, MERIDIAN
and NAL BOOKS are published by NAL PENGUIN INC.,
1633 Broadway, New York, New York 10019

First Printing, December, 1987

1 2 3 4 5 6 7 8 9

PRINTED IN THE UNITED STATES OF AMERICA

1

The *Hendron Messenger*, a CCP, was three blinks and almost ten parsecs out of Tigian II bound New Earth when the Panic Flash from X&A Headquarters on Xanthos began to travel all recorded blink routes in the Andromeda sector of U.P. space. The *Hendron Messenger*'s automatics recorded the Panic Flash and sent an alert to the officer on watch, Captain Janos Black. Black pulled himself up from an alcohol-deepened sleep and, only half dressed, made his way to the bridge.

Any alarm in deep space is, without a play on words being intended, alarming. The *Hendron Messenger*, cargo carrier perishable, was not a new ship. Black's thick, gray hair was standing on end literally and figuratively until he saw that it was only a message. He brushed back his tousled hair, tugged his trousers into a more comfortable conformation over his paunch, and sat down at the console with a sigh. Probably, he was thinking, just more panic from the home office. He had never lost a cargo, even when it was as critically perishable as tani fruit, a rich man's delicacy that grew only in the temperate zones of the multi-sunned Tigian II.

Black punched buttons and the message printed itself across the screen and he jerked into instant indecision. A Panic Flash from X&A was, for any ship in space, an order to be obeyed at the risk of the most severe penalties known in space law. He had, he knew, only one choice, and that was to obey.

But Janos Black was one week short of retirement. He had, for five decades, sunk his bonus and retirement pay into Hendron Unlimited stock, and he was just one week away from drawing out his nest egg and starting the best part of his life, retirement on a new and beautiful little planet where imported money was not taxed and other laws, including those regarding the hidden ownership of females not registered as citizens of the U.P., were equally favorable to a man of somewhat odd tastes. Black owned enough Hendron stock to sit on the board of directors, and he knew that the company's financial position had deteriorated after the death of old Evan Hendron, the company's founder. He'd seen things go from good to not so good and then to risky, risky enough to induce Black to file for retirement at the end of his current trip. Things were, he knew, so bad that the loss of his cargo—Evan Hendron would never have risked carrying such an expensive and perishable commodity—would make it possible for one disgruntled creditor to ruin fifty years of savings. The stock of a company in receivership would be worthless, and that would leave Black no choice but to rot aboard such space tramps as the *Hendron Messenger* for the rest of his life.

Black made his decision within seconds of seeing the message flash on the screen. He, being the captain of the ship, had the only emergency access key to the ship computer's sealed chambers. He, like all licensed ship's captains, had had his required training in computer repair. It was but the work of minutes for him to be probing into the computer's recording chambers. He knew that he was breaking the law, for the computer's recorder was the ship's log, but he had already bought a thousand acres along the shore of a clear-water lake, had plans drawn for the retreat which would serve him for the balance of his life, and he'd be long gone, his stock sold and his life's savings safely liquid before the company ran a routine check on the *Hendron Messenger*'s log to find the tampering.

Next, he removed the keyed cover from the communicator, hurt one small chamber, resealed the communicator, and leaned back. He punched up the repeat of the X&A Panic Flash, got, as he had planned, garbage, and then, with a satisfied smile, sent to the nearest blink station ahead a request for a repeat of the message just sent down the line. Because of his work on the communicator, the repeat was the same as the one that was on the screen, garbage.

Meanwhile, the blink generator was building charge for the next leap down the established blink routes, and that blink would remove the

Hendron Messenger from the sector of space affected by X&A's Panic Flash. Any one of his three crewmen could find and repair the hurt to the communicator rapidly, but by that time the *Messenger* would be so near New Earth that there'd be no question of her blinking back to a small planet hundreds of parsecs away.

Captain Janos Black was relieved on watch by his number three, a young man just three years out of the Merchant's Space Academy on Xanthos.

The *Hendron Messenger* was a casual ship. Company uniforms were worn, but the four men aboard, including the captain, could come up with colorful and comfortable adaptations of company attire. Aaron Delton had cut the legs off a pair of company white slacks, and the resulting shorts were topped by a loose, comfortable civilian shirt.

" 'Morning, Captain," Delton said. He was a throwback, in some ways, Janos Black thought, to earlier ages. At five feet ten inches, he was below average in height, and his face did not reflect his age. He had heavy, black hair that he allowed to become somewhat unruly while in space, but he was a good man, conscientious, easygoing, if not overly talkative.

"All nominal, Number Three," Black said, rising and scratching his paunch. "She's all yours."

Delton went to the dispenser and drew a mug of coffee, white, and sat down in the captain's chair. Black paused in the hatchway, still scratching his paunch. "You have a few minutes, after you finish routine cargo and systems checks, take a look at the communicator."

"Sure, Captain," Delton said. "What's the problem?"

"Probably nothing," Black said. "A blink came through garbage. Maybe military, scrambled, you know, but it won't hurt to check."

"I'll get on it, sir," Delton said.

First, however, there were the routines. Sensors in the cargo areas showed optimum temperatures and humidities. The precious cargo was reaching a peak of ripeness and would bring the highest prices on the docks at New Earth. All ship's systems were puttering along in the optimum as well. The checks went into the ship's log, mostly the computer talking to itself, and Delton sat, watching, savoring the good Tigian coffee.

Chores done, he opened the communicator hatch and attached monitors. It took five minutes to find the hurt chamber. If a man had wanted the communicator to garble an incoming blink message, Delton was thinking as he lifted the component board and inserted a spare that he'd taken from ship's stores, that was exactly the place to hurt the communicator. Odd, because that chamber was the heart of the receiver and had been engineered to be almost fail safe. In his experience he'd never known that particular component to fail.

He put the damaged unit under magnification in the ship's shop. He had expected to find the mark of an electrical arc, perhaps. He shook his head when he saw, instead, an indentation into soft metal. That would be one for the engineers to puzzle over, how metal trauma could occur in a closed chamber where there were no moving parts.

He recorded his finding into the ship's log, drew more coffee. They'd be on New Earth in less than a week, and he'd have two full months of leave. He smiled at the thought, because going home was the reward for months in space.

Aaron Delton was old to be a third officer on a merchant ship. He looked younger than his thirty-four years, but thirty-four was old: most academy men were third officers while still in their twenties. He had entered the academy at an age when most men were graduating, for he had made a basic mistake, early on, in his choice of careers. He'd spent a lot of time in laboratories before he had discovered that the life of a researcher, with its politics and restrictions, was not for him.

His education and experience in electronics and amino-acid memory chambers had not been totally wasted. If he couldn't advance computer science, he could absorb the knowledge that existed. His background in science had helped him breeze through the academy and then had immediately threatened to get him stuck in a planet-side job, for computer masters were in short supply. He had, however, held out against lucrative offers and signed on with the Hendron Company, and was now in line to be promoted to second officer after his current trip.

He had taken to space. Hendron ships traversed, mainly, well-traveled blink routes, in trade among the planets in the U.P. metro area, and he'd seen a lot of things he'd never have seen working in a lab. For a time the feel of new planets, and far places, had been enough. That was before he had met Tippy. As a married man, he now had a new goal, to move into the passenger liner trade and rise to captain, for the captain of a passenger liner had luxurious quarters and was allowed to have his family with him.

At the moment, however, he was not thinking of his family or of his future plans. As he finished his second cup of coffee he considered the problem of the bright, damaged metal in a place where *nothing* capable of doing that damage could have penetrated. He grunted, put aside the coffee cup, and, looking furtively over his shoulder, used a small, esoteric tool from a queer little gadget he carried always in his pocket to jimmy the fail-safe lock on the computer, then poked his head curiously into the computer's interior.

There were many things about Aaron Delton that his employers did not know, unless they had requested an X&A security clearance, not the usual thing for a merchantman officer. One of those things was the fact that Delton had spent years working on Century Series computers. In fact, it was Delton's inability to improve that venerable and widely used computer that convinced him that he was not an original thinker, and it was the boredom of it that had driven him to the space academy and into the lonely trade of space. What there was to be known, however, about a Century was known by Aaron Delton, and if his memory didn't contain it, he knew exactly where to find it in the ship's library.

In this case, he had no need to consult reference material. To his shock, he saw immediately that the ship's log had been altered, a criminal offense. That made him very curious. He got instruments from the locked captain's compartment in stores—the lock gave him no problem—attached them to the inner examination ports of the computer, and quickly located where an erasure had been performed, so sloppily that he had no trouble enhancing the echo image left after alteration. He saw the Panic Flash as originally received and his face went slack, his eyes opened wide, and he gave a hoarse shout. His hand lashed out to trigger the ship's alarm, a call for all officers.

The number-one and number-two officers arrived on the run, followed closely by a rumpled captain. By that time Delton had turned the ship, as she'd been lying on charge, waiting for the generator to be ready for another blink, and had programmed the longest blink he could compute in the direction of St. Paul, the only life-zone planet of a small star far outside the most traveled blink routes.

In spite of his personal agony, Delton had decided quickly not to confront the captain head to head. It was, of course, obvious that the captain had received the Panic Flash, had realized that it meant the loss of their perishable cargo, and had tampered with the ship's log. To accuse Black of that, however, would pit him against a ship captain's absolute authority. Better, he felt, to attack the captain obliquely in the presence of two other witnesses.

"Captain," he said, "I have programmed a blink toward the planet St. Paul, at the order of an X&A Panic Flash. That was the signal that came in garbled. I recovered it from an echo image in the computer. Permission, sir, to blink."

"Now hold on, Delton," Black said, panic making his voice high. "We're outside the alert sector. We're too far away."

"We weren't, sir, when the message was received," Delton said. "We're under space law, Captain." His finger went toward the blink button.

"Don't touch that button, Delton," Black said, and in his hand was his sidearm, a saffer that at the range of six feet, the distance between Black and Delton, would be a fatal weapon.

"Captain," Delton said, his finger poised, "St. Paul is my home. My wife and child are there."

Black paled. So that was why the name St. Paul had seemed familiar to him. But they were just three blinks out of New Earth and his retirement. "Delton," he said, "just how many passengers do you think we could put on this ship?"

"Captain, we are under a Panic Flash," Delton

said. He was growing more desperate with each wasted second.

"By the time we got there it would be over," Black said. "Every ship near that point in space is there. Your family has most probably already been removed to safety." His voice became more firm. "You will continue the course toward New Earth, Mr. Delton. It is my decision, as captain, that the ship is outside the alerted sector."

"Captain," said the first officer, "we were in the alert sector when the message was received."

"Garbled," the captain said. "We are now outside the alerted sector."

"Captain, as first officer, I advise compliance with the X&A order."

Black's eyes narrowed. "Are you challenging my authority, Number One?"

"Sir, I agree with the first officer," said the number-two man. "A Panic Flash takes precedence over all other considerations."

"We are going to New Earth," Black said. "Mr. Delton, push that blink button, now."

"Captain, log monitors are running, and have been since I called an alert," Delton said. "And I hereby officially refuse your order, on the grounds that it is illegal and against the directive of an X&A order."

"You may leave the bridge, Mr. Delton," Black said, swinging the vented muzzle of his weapon to point directly at Delton's chest.

"I go on record as being opposed," the number two said.

"Captain Black," said the first officer, "in accordance with space regulations, well known to all of us, I hereby declare that I, as first officer, am taking command of this ship, for the purpose of obeying an X&A Panic Flash. I remind you, sir, that this is being recorded into the log, and that I cite the priority of an emergency in space involving potential loss of life as my authority."

"Take one step toward me and I'll end this mutiny quickly," Black said as the first officer began to move toward him.

"I doubt, Captain, if you'll commit murder with the recorders going," the first officer said. "Now I'll have to ask you to give me your weapon."

In that instant, Black saw five decades of working and dreaming turning into cargo holds filled with rotten fruit and that was too much. He hardly realized that his finger was tightening on the trigger of the saffer until the flash engulfed the first officer.

"No," Delton yelled, leaping toward the captain just as the number-two officer, nearer Black, yelled and leaped to seize Black's arm and tilt the saffer toward the ceiling.

It happened in seconds. First there was the flash of the weapon and the first officer was falling, dead before he hit the deck, then the second officer's swift response and two men struggling, trying to keep their balance as they fought over possession of the saffer, with Delton, who had to move all the way around the control console, running to aid the second officer. So quickly. There had been four living men on the bridge when it began, and then, as Black lurched, lunged, pushed, put his chest hard against the second officer with the saffer pointed upward, held by the right hands of both men, the weapon flashed again at a moment when Black and the second officer were nose to nose. The flash caught both under the chin, deadened skin, muscle, and brain tissue, and it was over and there were three dead men on the *Messenger*'s deck.

It took Delton only seconds to check vital signs and assure himself that all three men were dead. He had never seen men die by violence, and he was shaking as he stood and moved swiftly back to the control console. He would, in accordance with space practice, put the three bodies into a cold room, but first he had things to do. His wife and child were on St. Paul. He used the charge in the *Messenger*'s generator and, while she recharged, dragged the bodies to a cold room, turned the temperature down, locked the door, and put an official ship's seal on the lock.

He slept fitfully, for a few minutes at a time, during recharging periods. The perishable cargo reached full ripeness and then began to rot and stink, the smell permeating the ventilation system. He discharged the entire cargo into space, millions of New Earth credits' worth of it, and continued the long, long blink trip, leaving the well-traveled ways, arching out into the periphery. He came out into normal space near a planet that he did not recognize. St. Paul had been a small planet, but blue and beautiful, and peaceful, and fruitful. St. Paul, his wife's planet of birth, had been a paradise. But no longer. She was now shrouded in an obscene cloud, a dark, impenetrable cloud.

All around him, in space, his detectors showed ships, large and small. The computer's emergency cooling system cranked in to dissipate the heat generated as the computer's full ability was put into action to place and avoid the largest congregation of space craft Delton had ever seen.

Delton opened up the close-range voice communicator and sent a call and was answered by the harried voice of a man of obvious authority, an X&A voice.

"The *Hendron Messenger*," Delton said. "I can accommodate at least twenty people."

"You're a little late, *Hendron Messenger*," the harried voice said. "Stand by, however. We'll use you to ease the overload on another ship."

"Commander," Delton sent, "how successful was evacuation?"

"Stand by, *Hendron Messenger*," the harried voice said.

"*Messenger*," another voice said, "This is *Calisto Miner*. I'm off your port quarter, low. We're overcrowded. We've got men and women sitting atop ore in the hold. You care to relieve us of a few?"

"*Calisto Miner*," Delton asked, "how total was evacuation?"

"It was a madhouse down there," *Miner* said. "Less than ten percent, some say."

Delton's heart went cold. But Tippy and his

son lived in the capital city. Surely the big city would have been a prime port of evacuation. "I am at rest, *Miner*," he said. "Please come alongside on the port. Main hatch is marked with the company logo."

It took a good half hour for the mining ship to maneuver into position, another hour to match the locks. Then the survivors began to come aboard. He took thirty of them, knowing that they'd be overcrowded, that the ship's supplies would run out quickly under that demand, but aboard *Calisto Miner* women and children still had to sit on the hard, rough ore in the holds.

He eased *Messenger* away from the mining ship, charted a short blast to clear the congestion near dust-shrouded St. Paul, then he joined the largest group of survivors in the crew's recreation room, the largest area aboard ship.

"Is there anyone here from St. Paul City?" he asked.

A small child was weeping weakly. Tired, soiled faces looked at him blankly.

"No one from the city?" he asked.

"We're mostly from the naval base," a man said. "There were riots in St. Paul City."

"Tell me," Delton said. "My wife and child lived in the city."

"It was bad," the man said. "It happened so suddenly. We had less than a week's warning. At first it was orderly. The existing ships began to ferry people out to the moon bases, and then it became apparent to everyone that there wasn't going to be time to get everyone off. The ships on Panic Flash alert began to join in the evacuation, and even then we knew that only a small percentage would make it. The riots started in St. Paul City, people battling to get aboard the available ships. At first there was holo coverage, and as we waited at the naval base for our turn we saw them go wild in the city. Women and children were trampled, brained with clubs. Men fighting to get into the loading ramps. The police used stun guns and then more deadly force as they were attacked, and at the height of it the holo coverage went blank."

Delton's insides were chilled, as if by ice. He tried to picture Tippy's face, and could not. That, more than anything else, made panic boil up in him.

"Just before we go on a ship," another survivor said, "we heard an audio report from St. Paul City. It said that military and police were seizing all available space on the evacuation ships and that they were shooting civilians who tried to break through their lines."

Delton turned away, looked blankly at a bulkhead for long moments as he tried for control of his shaking hands. When he turned he seemed, at least on the surface, to be calm.

"Are there any qualified spacehands among you?"

Three men stood. One was the civilian captain of a navy tug.

"Good," Delton said. "I want you three men to join me on the bridge." On the bridge he saw that the three survivors who had shipboard experience were tired, soiled, but in relatively good condition. "Captain," he said to the tugger, "you will be number one. You"—he pointed to another man—"number two. You get on the communicator with that X&A ship and find out where we should take these people. Number three, I suggest that you do your best to get the survivors as comfortable as we can make them in our limited space, dole out a short ration of food, and then get some rest."

The new number three moved swiftly off the bridge. Delton said, "Keep the watch, Number Two. Number One, please come with me." He led the way into the generator room, the only place he had not placed survivors. "Captain," he said, "are you familiar enough with a ship of this type to take responsibility for her?"

"I am," the man said. "I see you wear the insignia of a third officer. Where is your captain and the rest of the crew?"

"Captain, you'll see that I have sealed the number-one cold room, and the ship's log as well. When you discharge your passengers, please notify Hendron's nearest office of your whereabouts and then call an X&A investigations officer. He will find all events aboard this ship recorded in the log by sound and visual monitors."

"The rest of the crew is dead, then?"

"Yes."

"Perhaps I should exercise my authority as a ship's captain and put you in confinement until X&A has a chance to investigate.'

"No," Delton said. "My wife and child were down there. I didn't kill the captain and the officers." He had his hand on the saffer he'd taken from the captain's dead hand. "The ship is yours for the moment, Captain," he said. "I have something I must do."

Launches aboard all U.P.-registered merchant vessels met critical X&A standards. They were used, most often, as the captain's gig, but they were provisioned to keep all crewmembers well and alive for an extended period in deep space; thus, they were also lifeboats, and had interstellar blink capacity. The *Hendron Messenger*'s launch was newer than the mother ship, herself the latest in U.P. technology, safer, the crew had often said, than the *Messenger*, and capable of traveling as far and as fast.

The tugboat captain on the bridge of the *Messenger* felt the displacement as the launch separated from the ship, flipped on an external viewer, and saw the launch fall away toward dust-shrouded St. Paul.

"Poor son-of-a-bitch," he muttered.

"He's going down," said one of the other survivors. "Kill himself, sure."

Aaron Delton was going down. He used the full capacity of the launch's sensors and lowered the small but powerful ship into the dust cloud that filled the planet's atmosphere. At one hundred thousand feet the launch encountered severe turbulence, then a sky that seemed solid with muddy rain.

Visibility zero. Turbulence. A storm that outdid any storm Delton had ever experienced. And still he drove the launch down, down, watching sensors, knowing that all charts of St. Paul were now obsolete and worse than useless, for to use a chart would mislead him.

He actually touched the wind-flattened tops of sixty-foot waves before he could see surface, and then only by the use of powerful floods. Three times, as he searched for a recognizable landmark, a mountain, a city, he came near death.

They had called the warnings about St. Paul's instability the cryings of Cassandras. Other planets were more instable, and had a longer history of instability than St. Paul, and in the history of the exploration of space no planet had given in to that instability. The accumulation of ice at the poles, the scientists said, was normal, a periodic climate change that had been repeated often in St. Paul's remote past. Before the instability became critical, the government said, measures would be taken to melt some of the burden of ice making the planet unbalanced. There was, they had said, plenty of time. Ages of time. No worry. No problem.

The launch eased up and over a mountain range on sensors. The mini-computer identified the slightly altered profile of a peak. Delton's heartbeat increased. Already ice was forming below as he hugged the ground past the mountains. Mighty forests had been leveled. There was a tossing sea where once there had been fruitful agricultural plains, the waters of that sea beginning to freeze, for now the sea was the planet's north pole, and there, on the shores of that sea, toppled, crumpled, was the city. Visibility, there at the far north, was improved, for all moisture in the air was being condensed and frozen, gathering the clouds of dust to make dirty snow, and the city was being slowly obliterated. The temperature outside was fifty below, and the still disturbed atmosphere made for winds of hurricane force. Windblown ice and dust particles acted as an abrasive on the launch, marring paint, leaving marks on the viewports. There were no survivors of St. Paul City.

The Department of Exploration and Alien Search was, perhaps, the most efficient agency in human history. As the *Hendron Messenger*'s launch cleared murky atmosphere, organization was already well underway, the fleet of varied vessels being assigned planets of destination, a census being taken at the same time. Soon the lists of survivors were being broadcast on various bands.

At the far rear of the fleet, as it began to move away from St. Paul, the small launch went unnoticed on detectors. The launch followed the fleet until the list of survivors was complete and the list had been checked and rechecked by the Launch's mini-computer. The names of Tiffany Delton and Aaron Delton II did not appear on any list, from any of the thousands of ships. One thing was evident, as Delton programmed the mini-computer for a search of the names of those evacuated from St. Paul City. The overwhelming majority of survivors of the city were male, and members of either the military or the police.

One man who had not been on St. Paul was listed as missing and presumed dead. The third officer of a merchant ship had taken the ship's launch in a futile and desperate search for his missing wife and child. It was, for Delton, a moment of bemused and dazed wonder. He didn't feel dead. He felt the death of his wife and son, and that made a part of him dead, but a part of him was alive and helpless in the face of cosmic disaster. And then he began to put together all the things he'd heard. Something had gone very wrong on St. Paul. The fabric of civilization had been strained by the threat of sure death, and that fabric had ripped, making a vent through which his wife—ah, Tippy—and his son had fallen.

At that moment, in all the known universe, there seemed to be nothing worthwhile. He let the launch drift, did not think of food, drink, or his own personal comfort for long hours. Atop the great wrench he felt continuously there was an additional sadness. Everything that had happened aboard the *Hendron Messenger* had happened for nothing. Three men were dead and, less importantly, but of definite effect on the lives of many, a company would be in dire financial straights, and for nothing. The survivors he'd taken aboard would have been uncomfortable aboard the mining ship, but they would have survived. For nothing, and there was nothing he could do to alter any of the events. Unless. Unless. A germ of an idea began to form. His life, he felt, was over for all practical purposes. Anything he chose to do would be mere make-do, motion for the sake of movement.

Unless. Unless.

Janos Black had not killed his wife and son. If the *Messenger* had blinked immediately after receiving the Panic Flash, it would have arrived too late. He could blame Black only for the death of two men with whom he'd worked for a few months, men who were not close enough to him to be called friends, but men, nevertheless. Did Black's murderous stupidity justify what he had in mind, stealing Hendron property? Well, he thought, what the hell. One small ship's launch wouldn't matter much, compared to the value of the ruined cargo. He could even rationalize that Hendron, or someone, owed him that much, for he had lost his all, and so, the germ of an idea began to grow as he searched the chart bin and selected his route and sent the launch blinking away from the rescue fleet toward the far rim.

2

John Madison had to wear multiple hats in the office of Dunking Deep Space Ltd. on Pandaros. He was a shipping agent, on those rare times when a Dunking chartered freighter docked at the one port on Pandaros. He was a commercial diplomat, the representative of a firm whose reputation was not exactly galaxy wide among the business community. He was dispatcher for Dunking's three deep-space tugs based on Pandaros, and he was office manager, home-office liaison, personnel manager, and crew procurement officer.

Of all Madison's headaches, most of them brought on by the simple fact that Pandaros was not exactly a U.P. metro planet, crew procurement was the most nettlesome. In the first place, very few qualified tug men ventured into the outback, that wisp of stars far out on the edge, far past Old Earth and at the greatest distance from the clustered glory of the U.P. with Xanthos at the center. In the second place, few men in their right minds wanted to stay on Pandaros, whose chief claim to existence was a barely breathable atmosphere rich in sulfur and the most varied assortment of native animal life this side of the dim, almost forgotten, and surely distorted history of Old Earth before the destruction.

Deep-space tugs were assigned to specific stations along blink-routes, the routes so laboriously charted by X&A over the centuries of deep-space travel, by bids. Not even the most crusty legal beagle in Dunking's home offices on New Earth could tell Madison—although he'd long since lost interest—the origin of the curious system of deep-space rescue and salvage. The general understanding was that it went far back into Old Earth history, when surface travel by sea was a major form of transport. Whatever its origin, the system was deceptively simple.

Ships traversed space. Ships were mechanical and electronic. Things mechanical and electronic break down. When a ship broke down in deep space, it had to be towed to a repair facility. Someone had to do the towing, and there what was known as the ancient system of free enterprise came into play. In the early days of deep space there had been deep-space tugs, and it had been, according to a couple of interesting books Madison had read, quite a free-for-all, because the system then was that the first tug to get a tractor beam on a disabled ship reaped the financial rewards, usually a percentage of the disabled ship's worth, cargo included. As a result of the early system, the deep-space tugs congregated on well-traveled routes, often shouldering each other in an effort to be first on scene.

The system had become more orderly as the blink routes were extended into the infinity of the galaxy. Now regulations defined specific areas to be covered by a tug of a specific class, and each assigned tug post along all blink routes was let by open bid. The more frequented the blink route, the more desirable the post, so the deep-space salvage business was a very competitive one. The big outfits could cut their margin of profit per ship to the bone and, thus, the big outfits, like Xanthos Towing Ltd., always bid lowest on the highly desirable, densely traveled routes and they got most of the gravy.

Deep-space tugs were a relatively unimportant subsidiary of Dunking Deep Space Ltd. Dunking's total fleet of tugs wouldn't equal in number what Xanthos Towing had on post within ten parsecs of U.P. center, and Dunking didn't bid low. As a result, Dunking's tugs were on station in far places. If you listened to the men who manned Dunking's fleet, you'd think that the galaxy had multiple orifices of a specific type and that Pandaros, home port of Dunking's *D. H. Dunking, Emily X. Dunking,* and *Lareina Rule Dunking* was, anally, at the top of the orifice list.

John Madison liked it well enough on Pandaros. He was not an outdoor man. He rarely ventured into the sulfuric atmosphere, and Dunking Deep Space Ltd. had not stinted on air filters in the office and his adjoining quarters, where he shared his bed with his wife of forty years, who was happy as long as the regular mail ship brought the latest holo tapes from the more sophisticated U.P. planets. What Madison didn't like was that the *Emily X. Dunking* was lying dockside, her assigned post on an out-galaxy blink route temporarily unguarded, and only one crewmember available to man her.

For months he'd been sending regular reminders to the home office that he'd exhausted his small pool of qualified men who were willing to work for the low wages paid by Dunking and on the rather vain hope, considering the lack of traffic on Dunking's posts, of share money after a tow. For months he'd been ignored, and now he had a tug idle, with only two days of downtime pay coming from X&A before the *Emily X*'s contract became null and void. He wasn't particularly worried about losing the post, because last bid time Dunking had offered the only bid for the posts off Pandaros, but he was worried about what some computer hack would say back in the home office when it was discovered that a perfectly good deep-space tug was idle for lack of crew. About the only good thing about the Dunking tug operation on Pandaros was the fact that the three tugs were second generation Mules, the state of the art in deep-space tugs, and Madison had so few things in which to take pride that he didn't want to lose a tug.

So when his native-born secretary announced, in her unique Pandaros accent, that a spacer wanted to see the employment officer, Madison didn't even attempt to play it cool. He met the job applicant at the door with a warm hand-

shake and a good denture smile and had a cup
of coffee in the man's hand within seconds. Only
then did Madison take time to examine the man.
He was of less than average height, had close-
cropped black hair, and looked to be under thirty.
He had none of the telltales of the drinker or the
drugger, but one could never tell without a quick
lab test, which Madison would have to demand.
If the man turned down the test, it was an admission of the use of some controlled or illegal
substance and an automatic end to his chances
of working for Dunking.

"Thank you for seeing me so quickly," the
man said.

"No problem," Madison said. "My secretary
said you're a spacer."

"I've been running a private messenger service in a small private yacht," the man said. "I
guess I'm not cut out to be a businessman. I
made enough to eat, but not enough to keep the
yacht in license. I sold her on Titian last month.
Heard that Dunking might need tug hands."

"We'll be glad to take your application, Mr.—"

"Andrews," the man said. "They call me Tob.
You'll find the full name, if you're interested, in
here."

Andrews leaned forward and dropped a standard spaceman's leather credentials folder in
front of Madison. The leather showed little sign
of wear. Madison opened the folder. There was
the standard Z card, red, white and blue, with
the official seal of X&A. It, like the leather folder,
was unworn and the issue date was just two

years in the past. The spacer's service log was next to be examined. The log showed three years of ownership of a private yacht operated as a messenger in a thinly planeted sector a quarter of the way across the galactic disk from Pandaros. Before that Andrews had served as third officer on various merchant vessels, after being promoted officer from union spaceman's ranks.

"A mustang, huh?" Madison asked, a bit disappointed that the job applicant had neither formal merchantman's training nor fleet or X&A experience.

"That's it," Andrews said, giving Madison the impression that he didn't care much whether or not he got the job.

"Well," Madison said, not about to let the man get away, "the private experience is impressive. You must know how to navigate to cover the space you covered."

"I'm alive," Andrews said, with a thin smile.

"Obviously," Madison said. "I see no next of kin listed."

"No."

"No home address."

"I don't expect anyone to be looking for me."

"I do hope that no one in the law enforcement field will be looking for you here," Madison said, raising his eyes to see the man's reaction. "You'll have no objection, of course, to drug tests and a retinal scan for identification?"

"None," Andrews said.

"Hum. I do wish you had some tug experience."

Andrews shrugged.

"We can't give you an indoctrination course," Madison said. "Frankly, Andrews, I'm in a bit of a bind."

"I saw the tug at dock."

"Can you handle it?"

"I understand that a Mule is manned by two people," Andrews said. "You're talking as if my fellow crewmember has no more experience aboard tugs than I do."

Madison cleared his throat. Andrews smiled. "Perhaps you'd like to meet the other crewmember?"

"Why not?"

Madison opened his office communicator and spoke softly into it. "She'll be here in ten minutes, Mr. Andrews. In the meantime—"

"She?" Andrews asked, leaning forward with a frown.

"Her qualifications are perfectly in order," Madison said. "In fact, they're more impressive, in some ways, than yours. She was second officer aboard a passenger liner working the central worlds. She's a graduate of the Merchant's Space Academy and—"

Andrews was on his feet. "No," he said. "I won't spend six months at a time in space with a woman."

Madison felt quick panic, seeing his shiny new tug blinking away from Pandaros to become the charge of some other Dunking manager at a more profitable site. He held up his hand. "At least see her, talk with her." He smiled suggestively. "You might change your mind once you see her."

"No deal," Andrews said "Find a qualified man and I'm with you. Otherwise—" He turned, started toward the door. The door opened and the secretary was there.

"She happened to be in the waiting room," the secretary said as a tall, slim, dark-haired beauty stepped past her, smiled quickly at Madison, and then looked at Andrews with a pair of eyes that were nothing less than spectacular.

The history of mankind was well documented from the beginning of the second space age, but disappeared into dim legend prior to the push outward from the original core of the United Planets. The home planet of the race, Old Earth, had been rediscovered just over two centuries past, and archaeological research on that devastated planet added, and continued to add, to man's knowledge of his origins. Among the more astounding discoveries on Old Earth was the existence of many languages, many separate racial types, and a diversity of animal and plant life that had made the Earth the jewel of the galaxy.

To the best knowledge of archaeologists and historians, two basic racial types had begun the first outward push from Old Earth before the destruction, possibly in a joint effort, and as a result mankind had become homogenized. It was very unusual to see what Tob Andrews saw as the tall, lithe girl in a tight coverall singlet entered the room, a glimpse, perhaps, into the rich diversity of human types on Old Earth, for she had skin darker than the most dangerous suntan, skin that glowed with an inner life. She had a heavy shock of dark, thick hair piled atop her head in artful carelessless. Her black eyes were wide-set, and the upward tilt at the outer corners was emphasized by her makeup.

"Captain Andrews," Madison said, "this is Space Officer Nema Samira."

Each of the two, Andrews and the girl, glanced quickly at the agent, for in his introduction he had clearly stated the proposed relationship aboard the tug.

The girl had a businesslike walk. She had the body to be showcased by swaying, but she swayed not, walked straight and firm, high heels clicking on the dura-tile floor, to offer her hand to Andrews. Her grasp, too, was businesslike, not feminine, and her dark eyes met his without hesitation or flutter.

"I'm so pleased that you've completed the crew, Mr. Madison," she said, dropping Andrews' hand. "Have you told Captain Andrews the conditions to be observed aboard ship?"

Madison cleared his throat.

"That won't be necessary," Tob said. "I won't be aboard the tug, Officer Samira."

Madison spread his hands. "Captain," he said, "won't you please at least talk with Officer Samira?"

"Officer Samira," Tob said, "it's nothing personal, but I don't choose to share close quarters for six months with a woman."

Nema's sloe eyes narrowed, flashed dark fire. "I need this job, Captain," she said. "I will not thrust my femininity upon you. In fact, I was about to tell you that a condition of my contract is that if my crewmate is male he will be required to sign an agreement of privacy. We will see each other only at change of watch. If you can honor such an agreement, I assure you that you will not be burdened by my female presence either during your watch or on your off-time."

Tob was doing some quick thinking. He had a few hundred thousand universal credits saved, most of the sum having come from the sale of his boat. His plans had not exactly been soaring toward completion, mostly because he had found that the way he'd chosen to accumulate operating capital had not been particularly profitable. He hadn't even made enough with his private messenger service to do the required checks and maintenances on his boat. If he didn't take this job, he'd have to spend some of his nest egg looking for another, and he couldn't afford to waste any more time—not after all the useless years already behind him.

His personal reasons for not wanting to be exposed to a woman, and a beautiful one at that, could be subsumed by his overall purpose. In fact, when he thought of it from a coldly practical standpoint, a woman's relative lack of physical strength would make things easier when and if the time came to move toward easing the drive that had been pushing him for three years.

"Let me see the agreement," he said.

Madison dug into a file and quickly handed

him a sheaf of papers. "It's rather long and involved, Captain," he said. "Basically, it states that any male crewmate of Officer Samira's is bound by her right of privacy and that any sexual advances will result in both civil and criminal procedures. The agreement also requires that monitors be used constantly so that holo records will be available in the event of any invasion of Officer Samira's privacy."

"All right," Andrews said. "Have your legal beagle draw up one exactly like it for me, with the proper changes to include my name and my sex."

The dark girl's face darkened further in a flush of anger, but she held her tongue. "That is agreeable with me," she said.

"Good, good," Madison said heartily. "The agreement will be ready this afternoon, Captain. As you both know, the *Emily X* is provisioned and ready. Perhaps you'd like to look over the list of stores to see if there's any small delicacy that you'd like to add to food stores. And my office computer is tied into the Pandaros Central Library so that you may choose your reading and entertainment needs, in addition to the standard library aboard ship. If you'd like some help there, my wife will be glad to assist you. She's rather an expert on entertainment tapes."

"I have my own library," Nema said.

"If your wife will be so kind," Tob said, "have her select recent holos in the action and adventure field."

"She'll be happy to," Madison said. "There's one other matter, Captain Andrews. Officer Samira has had her medical. If you'll stop by the clinic—"

"No problem," Tob said. "I'll do that first thing, and then Officer Samira and I will have a look at the tug."

The medical consisted mainly of a blood and urine test for drug or alcohol use. It was a short trip by ground car to the docks, where the *Emily X. Dunking* sat squatly on her pad, impressively rugged in design, the shape and square bulk of her speaking of the power of her generator. She had a gleaming new paint job. The entrance hatch opened to the code Madison had given to Tob. He entered first, Samira following.

A Mule II was a compact ship, a triumph of design, and a near miracle in the use of limited space. Much of her was taken up by her massive blink generator, a source that produced enough power to allow her to move the largest ship in space over infinite distances. More space was devoted to stores. Crews quarters, on opposite sides of and opening into the control bridge, were pleasantly spacious and luxurious. One perk of being a tugger was that no expense was spared to make life bearable during the long months of boredom and inaction for the two men, or in this case man and woman, aboard. Each crewman's cabin was equipped with a computer terminal tied into the main ship's computer, with the state of the art in holo and music reproduction. The ship's automated galley turned out meals ranging from the native foods of a hundred planets to the sophisticated cuisine of the metro U.P. worlds.

Tob, after inspecting the captain's cabin with an approving smile, came back onto the bridge and made some quick checks of ship's systems, stores, ship's library, and began to familiarize himself with the control console. The girl came out of her cabin and stood looking over his shoulder.

"Looks good to me," Tob said. "Want to play with her for a while?"

"I've spent the last two days in familiarization," Nema said. "Once my private library is aboard I am ready." She looked at him musingly for a moment. "Madison didn't mention that the liquor cabinet has not been restocked from the last trip. Apparently the last crew made the most of it, because the stock is exhausted."

"Will you handle that, please," Tob said. "Some Tigian white wine for me. A couple of cases of a decent brandy. Whatever you want for yourself."

Nema nodded, pleased to find that her captain was not a heavy drinker. "I will," she said, turning to the communicator to give crisp orders to the clerk in Dunking's supply room. Tob opened the computer and ran a test problem in navigation, found the computer to be in perfect working order. Men began to arrive with Tob's personal things. He directed the placement of them in his cabin. Nema had been inspecting the well-equipped recreation room. More men arrived with her things and she began to feed her personal holo and music tapes into the ship's library, the task facilitated by software that was added to the computer's chambers in one simple operation.

Mrs. Madison, a grandmotherly lady with a bright face and a sunny smile, came aboard followed by a young man with a large crate of holo tapes. "I think you'll find some very good stuff here, Captain," she said, after shaking Tob's hand and introducing herself. "I do hope so. And I pray that you'll have a pleasant and profitable tour."

"You're very kind," Tob said. "When we take a Lloyd's on a disabled passenger liner and I get my prize money, I'll buy you a Selbelle fire ruby."

Mrs. Madison laughed. "I'll hold you to that, young man. You heard that, didn't you, Miss Samira?"

"I'm your witness," Nema said.

The liquor arrived and was dispensed into the ship's system. It was darkfall on Pandaros. The *Emily X* was buttoned up, automatics humming and clicking, temperature and humidity optimum through her living quarters.

"I'm spending the night aboard," Nema announced, thinking that Tob, being a male, would want to spend his last night planetside sampling the pleasures of Pandaros' social life.

"I'd planned to do the same," Tob said.

The voice of John Madison came from the caller. Nema, answered. "Ah, Officer Samira," Madison said. "Is everything in order?"

"We're ready to go," Nema said.

"Excellent," Madison said. "My wife and I will come down to see you off tomorrow morning."

"Hold on a minute," Tob said to Nema, who closed the transmit switch and looked at him inquiringly. "I'd just as soon sleep in space. Have you any objections?"

"None," she said.

Tob took the caller. "Madison, any objections to our leaving tonight? We can be on station twelve hours earlier that way."

"What a splendid idea," Madison said, obviously pleased. "No objections at all."

"We'll see you in six months, then," Tob said. He closed the caller, began to punch up power into the thrusters, sent power into the blink generator. The ship seemed to take on a new life. A barely perceived hum, a living statement of continued function of vital systems that would become a part of them in the next six months, began.

"I want you to take her up and through the first couple of blinks," Tob said. "I'll be here with you."

Nema started to protest. "I understand," she said. "You want to see if I'm capable of operating a Mule."

"I'll give you the same chance to check me out, if you like."

"Perhaps," she said, taking the captain's chair while Tob moved to one side. She contacted Pandaros control. There was no delay in getting clearance. Pandaros Port was not exactly busy in the early evening. Nema's fingers flew as she gave instructions to the computer. She was very facile, but how good was she? Pretty good, he concluded, when the *Emily* lifted on flux drive without a vibration or a jerk and accelerated into the sulfurous atmosphere. He watched closely as she programmed the first three blinks. *Emily*'s generator was so huge, so powerful, that it could move the tug through multiple blinks without a halt for recharge. Nema blinked the ship just as she cleared dense atmosphere and within a few seconds, with two more blinks following immediately, *Emily* was a mote in the total blackness of deep space, parsecs from Pandaros, three right-angle blinks from her station.

"I assume," Nema said, "that you follow recommended procedure."

"If I know what it is," Tob said.

"It's standard operating procedure not to drain the generator completely, to keep a reserve in the event of a sudden emergency call."

"Makes sense to me," Tob said, although he realized that there were two chances of *Emily*'s receiving an emergency call—slim and none.

"Recharging," Nema said, kicking the computer into auto and turning to face Tob. "How did I do, Captain?"

"Looked good to me," Tob said. "Do you like six or twelve-hour watches?"

"I prefer twelves," she said.

"Okay. We'll be on station before midnight."

The tug's clock would hold Pandaros time, although, of course, night and day meant nothing in space. "What do you say I take the first one, give you a chance to start out fresh after a sleep period?"

"I ask no special consideration," she said evenly.

"Nor will you get it," he said. "While we're charging, we'll run another check on all systems."

"All right," she said.

It began. Mostly it was the computer humming and clicking, with Nema's fingers flying over the punchboard now and then. She spoke in a deep, businesslike voice. "Air repurification system, check. Heaters, check."

When the ship's check was complete, it was eleven o'clock. "Coffee?" Tob asked.

"Ummm, yes," Nema said, starting to rise.

"I'll get it."

"White for me."

"Me too." He brought her coffee and leaned against the console. "What sort of name is Samira?"

She shrugged. Under her coverall singlet her shoulders were slim, her waist tapering, her breasts full. "Like many, my family had its own family lore. We fancy our line to be very old. It can be traced back to the original planet of settlement in the Zede system." She gave him an unconscious smile. "But don't come up with any of that corny rebel stuff. Our family was almost wiped out during the war, fighting on the side of the U.P."

"A family that keeps a name for a thousand or more years must be something," he said.

"Oh, in family lore, we go further back than that, to Old Earth. The original Samira in space is reputed to have come from one of the Old Earth's most ancient civilizations."

"I'm in the presence of a blue blood," Tob said.

She laughed. She seemed at ease. There was none of the formal stiffness about her that she'd displayed in the Dunking office. "There was rejoicing when I was born with those large, slanted eyes and dark skin. I was a throwback, proof of our bloodline. Women who looked like me have been found pictured in ancient rock inscriptions in the ruins of the Old Earth."

"Interesting," he said, glancing at his watch. "And why are you out here in the tail end of nowhere?"

"That's not your concern," she said evenly, with a tight little smile.

"Sorry," he said. "We're charged. You may put us on station, Officer Samira."

"Aye, aye," she said, turning to send the *Emily* blinking, then blinking again at right angles, followed the established routes, passing by the small, lonely blink beacons that marked the march of a civilization to and through the stars. After the third blink she checked her coordinates carefully, noted that Tob was double-checking behind her. If they saw two ships in the next six months they'd consider it a busy tour, but it wouldn't do for *Emily* to be lying dead in space directly in the blink route.

When the tug was positioned to the side of the route, but still close enough to intercept any messages and to detect the signal that a blinking ship sends ahead of itself, she put the tug into auto, rose, glanced at the chronometer, and said, "Right on time, Captain." It was two minutes to twelve.

"Well done," he said. "I'll take her now. Good night."

She hesitated upon leaving, then turned and spoke from the hatchway into her quarters. "I'm sorry if I seemed rude. There are just certain things I don't care to discuss."

"No problem," he said, for he, too, had things he did not care to discuss with anyone.

Alone, he drew coffee, adjusted the control chair to his contour, and listened to the regulated and reassuring purrings and mutterings of the living ship around him. Six months. He looked at the chronometer. Less than thirty minutes had passed. Six months could be a long, long time. He sighed, leaned forward, and punched directions into the computer. The book he choose was the work of a savant at Xanthos University, a huge, dry tome dealing with man's various experiments in government.

3

During her watch, Nema liked to orient the *Emily* so that her largest bridge viewport showed the disk of the galaxy as a wide, silver band across the blackness. She rarely looked at the emptiness behind her, for there the stars thinned, and most of those visible were distant galaxies. Beyond Pandaros, there were only a handful of discovered life-zone planets, none with the type of planetary riches to attract large populations.

As if to belie the remoteness of the *Emily X*'s assigned post, two ships passed within the first month, one outbound, one a space-darkened tramp merchantman, making her way back toward Dunking's ports on Pandaros. The incoming ship lingered near *Emily*'s blink beacon, eagerly accepting the latest news holos from *Emily*'s computer, reports that by that time were, as far as news from the metro areas of the galaxy were concerned, already months old. In her own turn, *Emily* recorded the news from the outbound ship, the ship having come all the way from a Zede world, laden with machine tools for an outplanet.

The passage of a ship from the more populated parts of the galaxy was, in Tob's opinion, reason enough to call his crewmate during her off-duty hours. When *Emily*'s detectors signaled the reception of the signal that flies seconds ahead of a blinking ship, and the tone indicated that the ship would rest for recharge within communication range, he pushed the call for Nema, expecting it to be some minutes before she could rouse from sleep, dress, and join him. Instead, she appeared immediately.

"Sorry to wake you," he said.

"You didn't," she said, her eyes taking in all boards to determine the reason for her off-duty summons.

"Ship, outbound," Tob said. "I thought you might enjoy some communication with other human beings."

"Thank you," she said, as the ship's hailer began to sound with a human voice and *Emily*'s official ship-to-ship hail code.

Together, they talked with the communications man aboard the outbound ship, and Tob cast a grin at Nema when she first spoke and the voice on the hailer said, "Ah, a lady."

Nema frowned and made no acknowledgment of the man's surprise. She requested the latest news holos and they were beamed into *Emily*'s recorders while Tob and the communications officer aboard the outbound ship made small talk of planets visited, how things were back in U.P. central, and of the big black into which the ship was pointed.

"I can't understand why anyone would settle out here," were the communications officer's last words before the ship blinked and instantly put light-years between herself and *Emily*. Tob laughed. He felt good. His studies had become quite interesting. Sometimes he slept for his entire self-chosen six hours without dreaming. "Well, son," he said to the communications officer, who was long gone, "I wonder myself." He looked at Nema. "Why would anyone settle out here? For that matter, why would anyone live six months at a time on board a tug out here?"

Nema, too, had been stimulated by the brief voice contact with the race, but her smile faded and she looked at Tob with her dark eyes slitted. "Captain, if you're so keen on knowing my life history—"

Tob, surprised, raised his eyebrows. "My questions, Officer Samira, were more rhetorical than personal." He turned to the console, punched up an account of the Zedeian dictator whose ambition had started man's one war among the stars, and did not appear to hear when Nema slammed the door to her quarters.

The passages of the two ships were the only breaks in a routine that had been established quickly. The two crewmembers saw each other only at watch change, and their conversation became a series of repetitions, of phrases having to do with ship's operation. Sometimes the exchange was a brief as, "All systems nominal. No contact."

The only other times Tob saw Nema were

routinized, too. A few minutes after going off watch she would come out her door, dressed in leotards under a silken robe, and go into the recreation room where she spent two hours in exercise. When she was back in her quarters, the ship's instruments would record the running of her shower for what seemed to be, to Tob, a very long time. That presented no problem, for the ship's systems repurified all water, removing all foreign matter, such as soap, to be dumped periodically into space.

And so it went.

Until, in the sixth week, Nema failed for the first time to appear exactly five minutes before the start of her watch. Tob, finishing off a learned analysis of what little had been discovered about forms of government on Old Earth, didn't notice until the chronometer clicked the hour, and he was not then concerned. He would just continue reading in his quarters. But when a half hour went by and Nema had not appeared, he pushed her call button, waited another five minutes, pushed the call again, and then went to her door to ring the buzzer there. There was no response. He pounded on the door, shouted her name. The quarters were well soundproofed, and he doubted that she could hear his shouting. Puzzled, he pushed her buzzer for a long time and then began to be more concerned. He went back to the console and used the ship's communicator to send his voice, greatly amplified, into Nema's room, and still the door did not open.

He ran to get a coder from captain's stores,

ran back to the door to Nema's quarters, and applied the coder. It took only seconds for the little machine to find the personal code Nema had programmed into her lock and the door swung open to reveal a darkened room. Tob hit the lights and his heart leaped when he saw her. She lay on her back, a silken nightgown clinging to her wetly, her long hair lank with dampness, her face flushed almost bright red.

She was burning with fever. As he placed his hand on her damp forehead he had never felt anyone burn so. He tried unsuccessfully to rouse her. When he shook her shoulder, her body moved limply. He ran to the storeroom and seized the medical kit. Within a few seconds he knew that she was a very sick woman, with a fever of just over 103 degrees.

He applied contacts to her wrists, pushed down the filmy gown to reveal a breast of supreme beauty, placed another contact over her heart. A few more adjustments and the automated recorders in the medical kit showed her blood pressure to be dangerously low, her heartbeat slightly erratic.

Since it was not economically feasible to have a doctor aboard all spaceships, great advances had been made in automated diagnosis. The *Emily*, as state of the art in tugboats, had a medical unit. Tob carefully drew blood, having a bit of trouble finding a vein, so low was her blood pressure, and hurried to the bridge to activate the med unit. The computer muttered for only a few seconds and began to print out the diagnoses.

"Viral content of blood sample indicates with a probability of 100 percent that the subject is suffering from Pandaros six weeks fever, so called because of its long incubation period after exposure. Imperative that all personnel exposed have immediate injections of anti-Pandaros fever serum, unless symptoms which include sore throat, irritability, and shortness of breath have already begun."

Tob took a deep breath. He didn't feel irritable, his throat was not sore, and he breathed normally.

"Treatment of subject is to be as follows," the computer printed, and Tob waited until the printout was completed before he ripped it off and made a run for the medical stores.

He lowered his pants and popped a self-spray injection of the serum into his right buttock, as directed, then began to gather the prescribed medicines and materials needed for treatment of a Pandaros-fever victim. One aspect of the treatment had made him gulp when he read it, but he ran back to Nema's room, hands full, and there was nothing to it but to do it. He gave her the first prescribed injection of antiviral drugs.

The fever was a serious matter, almost 100 percent fatal unless properly treated. He wondered why, as he began to follow the med unit's instructions, Madison had not suggested immunization. He felt lucky that he hadn't been on Pandaros earlier, but if Nema had been exposed, he'd probably been exposed. It was just that the six-week incubation period had not run out for him. The serum would prevent a full onslaught of the fever now.

But Nema was in a bad way. According to the med unit, her fever would remain high for hours before the antiviral drugs began to win the battle that was starting in her bloodstream. And that fever had to be prevented from becoming higher, lest she suffer brain damage.

That was the part that had made Tob gulp. He had to remove her sodden, silken nightgown and rub every inch of her body, a body that was surprisingly perfect and totally beautiful, with a fever reducer that both cooled the skin's surface and soaked deep down to cool beyond the layers of epidermis.

He had not seen a woman's body in over three years. He had not been able to bring himself to think of a woman in that length of time, had thought that he would never have the capacity to tolerate, much less want or love a woman ever again.

He cursed himself in colorful language from a hundred planets and from the frustrations of centuries of inventive spacegoers, for he could not divorce his mind from the firm softness, the smoothness, the beauty of that body, even though that body was burning with fever and the woman was in a coma.

And the fever reducer had to be rubbed on every hour for twenty-four hours, or until the fever began to drop below 100 degrees.

He was thankful when, after the third allover rub, the matter became routine with him. He was beginning to be a bit sleepy after six hours, and the fever had not broken. After ten hours the woman was nothing more than a sick human being who needed care. Still there was no change. It began to appear that it would take the full twenty-four hours for the drugs to begin to win the deadly battle, and he was tired. After finishing a rubdown and covering Nema's nakedness with a light sheet, he felt himself drifting toward sleep. He set the chronometer on her bedside table to awaken him, and dozed. He followed that pattern for two more hours and then, exhausted, fearful that not even the buzz of the alarm would awaken him, and having noted that Nema had begun to move her head now and then, he decided he'd try a bit of music to help keep him awake. He picked up Nema's remote unit from the table and punched a channel at random. Nema liked heavy drama. He checked several holo tapes and groggily pushed buttons. There appeared in the holospace a scene gleaming with gold and silver, rich fabrics, and a woman dancing to the richness of reeds and flutes. The music was odd, with a running rhythm that had a strange lilt. It was noise. He turned it up, his eyes glazed with lack of sleep, seeing, at first, only the luxury of the room in which the woman danced.

When he let his eyes find the dancing figure, aided as the image grew with the recorders zooming in, he saw long, sleek legs encased in diaphanous material, an exposed midriff that writhed with amazing muscular control, a set of proud breasts above a tiny waist, and a flow of dark, long hair hanging charmingly loose. And then, still half dazed with sleeplessness, he saw the face and he was instantly awake.

Nema was dancing, and her half–life-size figure was living in the holospace, three dimensional, perfect in color, so near that he could see the heave of breast as she breathed, the twirl of silk as she spun, the contortions of muscles in her stomach, and the writhing, swaying, very, very erotic and perfect hips. That, he realized, was the body he'd been rubbing, over every inch, for more hours than he liked to remember. That, he knew, was the most beautiful woman he'd ever seen, and that admission gave him so much pain that he punched the controls hard and the image disappeared immediately.

"As the fever begins to break," the med unit had written, "the subject will revive from deep coma with the possibility of delirium."

It was more than a possibility. Nema's temperature dropped a full degree and just as Tob was feeling relief she began to toss and mutter. At first she seemed merely restless, but as the hours passed she would toss her head violently, flail the bed with her arms, kick with her long and lovely legs, so that it was impossible to keep a cover on her and like trying to ride a rocket gone wild to rub on the fever reducer.

At first, her mumblings were just that, and totally unintelligible. After a while Tob began to catch isolated words, and as time went by and the chronometer showed that Tob had been treating her for twenty-two hours, he began to understand whole phrases. She talked of her mother, and of warm, family things, of summer and swimming. Then it all changed, with a shrill scream, and Tob shot upright in his chair, shocked. Her eyes were wide open.

"Hi," he said.

She saw nothing, or if she saw anything it was being projected from inside, from her memories, and she was screaming, "Mother, Mother."

The strength of her delirium scared Tob, and it was all he could do to hold her on the bed, and her words became a jumble, "No, no," being the only thing he could understand, and then, "Oh, not the children. Not the children. Stop them, stop them. What kind of men are you, stop them. The children!"

Once she sat up suddenly and seemed to look directly into his eyes. "I am not property," she said.

"Of course not," he said, but she did not hear, and was once again in that world of terror, screaming, yelling about the dying children, and then a rush of words that made Tob's heart stop, or so it seemed, for a moment.

"If I were a man, I would die on this planet rather than face your shame. If I have anything to do with it, the entire galaxy will curse you and the men of St. Paul forever."

Coming out of his shock, Tob shook her by the

shoulders. "What did you say? What did you say?"

"Mother, oh, Mother," Nema said, just before, exactly as predicted by the med unit, her delirium faded, her temperature dropped rapidly, and she fell into an even, peaceful sleep. The war of the bloodstream had been won by man-made drugs.

"Fever reducing rubdowns will continue until body temperature is normal," read the med unit printout, and Tob's arms were leaden, his eyes red as he covered Nema's body for the twenty-sixth time with his hands lubricated by the fever reducer. He had developed a system that saw the application of the reducer begin at her shoulders, work down to her feet, and then from the feet upward on the front, after he'd turned her over, to finish with her face and forehead.

He was gingerly applying the reducer to her soft-firm breasts when he almost lost his nose. He guessed, later, that she'd had the knife hidden under the edge of her mattress. The sharp point of it whizzed by his face even as he detected the swing of movement and the glint of metal and threw himself backward from the position in which he'd been straddling her thighs, fully clothed, in order best to apply the fever reducer.

"Goddamn," he yelled, using an ancient oath.

She had thrown herself after him, but she was weak, and the knife buried itself in the mattress inches short of his thigh and she fell back weakly.

"You animal," she hissed at him as he quickly leaped off the bed.

"You damned fool," he yelled at her. "If you've got enough damned sense, take a look at your precious monitors for the last twenty-six hours." Wherewith, he slammed her door behind him, not caring if she did have a relapse and not caring either if the entire X&A fleet flashed by and sent Panic Flashes, showered away his own sweat, remnants of the aromatic fever reducer, and flung himself, only half dry, into his bed to sleep for twelve hours.

He awoke, and his anger was still with him. He dressed and went onto the bridge. She was there, in her usual white coverall singlet, looking quite pale and weak.

"Get back in bed," he said harshly.

"I've only been up a few minutes," she said. "I checked. No action during the past thirty-eight hours."

"Fine," he said. "Now go back to bed."

"I checked the monitors."

"Fine."

"I'm sorry, Captain. I owe you thanks, not the blade of a knife."

"Forget the thanks, if you can forget the knife," he said ruefully, his anger fading. After all, she'd still been ill, not knowing what was happening.

She tried to laugh. "I have no secrets from you, do I?"

"At least none that are on the surface physically."

"Thank you. I assume you took the serum?"

"I did," he said. "That was mean stuff you had."

"I feel as if I've been used as a launchpad for a cruiser."

Tob looked at her for a moment. She was pale, and she seemed to have lost weight. "You've made it clear that you want no personal questions, and that's fine with me, but you said something while you were delirious. You mentioned St. Paul. Is that the planet, St. Paul?"

Her face darkened. "Why do you ask?"

He moved to thrust his face close to hers. "Look, I am not interested in you. I don't care about you. I don't care what or who you are or where you've been or why you're here on a tug or why you have such a low opinion of men. I do care about one thing, and I insist that you tell me why you mentioned St. Paul."

His intensity impressed her. Something concerning St. Paul was very important to him. "I was there when the planet shifted on its axis."

"Where?"

"St. Paul City."

"I want to know what happened, everything."

"I was performing there at the officer's club of the Area Seven-Four Military Operations Base."

"Obviously you got off the planet," he said, into a tense pause. "How did you manage that?"

"By promising certain favors to a few men in control," she said evenly. "I have not yet delivered on those promises, but I would have, had it been necessary. Have you ever faced certain death? Have you ever been in a position where there was no doubt that you'd die if you didn't do something?''

"I'm not interested in a discussion of philosophy.''

"When it became known that the imbalance was critical and that the last-minute efforts to melt polar ice would be too little too late, the general in charge of the base began moving people to the planet's moon on available ships. He moved the bulk of his own Space Commando Unit first. He justified that by saying that he'd need good, disciplined men to preserve order in the event of catastrophe. He told me that I could leave on a ship when it became possible to reserve space for dependents. He had his own private yacht standing by, just in case, but he said he didn't have room there for me.''

"And?'' Tob prompted.

"It became evident to me that I was expendable.''

"You're not making this very easy,'' he said. "Why do you say that you were expendable? Why you any more than millions of others?''

"Because I had come to St. Paul with the general,'' she said. "I thought he valued me. I found out how much. I discovered that the general was selling space on his ships, and on government ships under his control, for hundreds of thousands. The riots started, and he seemed to panic. He put his Commando at the fences and ordered them to open fire on anyone trying to force his way into the base. Meanwhile, I had been working to form my alliances with junior officers, with men I felt sure would be taken off. As I said, I made certain promises. One man got me aboard the last ship to leave the base. All around the base the few Commando who had not been taken off were working with police and other military units. They were using deadly force, lasers and saffers and stun smoke on civilians from the city. I saw them fire point-blank into groups of screaming women and children."

Tob had closed his eyes, imagining Tippy and his son caught up in a terrified crowd, almost hearing the sizzle of lasers, the crackle of saffers.

"The ship I was on was dangerously overloaded," she said. "We almost didn't make it. I was pushed up against a viewport and the ship was lifting so slowly. I saw a wave of police and Commando turn away from the fences, perhaps realizing they were going to be left. The civilians poured onto the base behind them. They swarmed all over the last ship on the ground and it didn't get off. Someone inside fired the flux drive and it incinerated dozens of people trying to force their way to the hatches, and then the engines stopped and people were still swarming over the ship when the planet began to shift. They put the sounds of it on the ship's communications system. It was unlike anything I'd ever heard. There was a great groaning, and the roar of winds and a crashing. The end of a world."

"This general of yours," Tob said, trying to concentrate on getting all available information instead of picturing Tippy and his son. "He said he needed troops to keep order after a world turned upside down?"

"His concern was saving a crack unit of Space Commando."

"And he was the one who first gave the orders to fire on civilians?"

"Yes. I happened to be with him when he laid down the policy."

"Why was he in charge? Where were the civilian authorities? St. Paul was a constitutional democracy."

"By default, I'd imagine," she said. "President Douglas made an inspiring speech in which he said that though his desire was to stay with his people, it was his duty to take the government off the planet so that it would be functioning when rescue efforts got under way."

"Who were they trying to kid?"

"That, initially, was what started the panic, the president and his government leaving. General Bender was the only authority there."

"Bender. That's your general?"

She nodded.

"Do you know who had responsibility for the commercial space ports around the city?"

"No. I watched news reports early on, and things were very orderly there. They were giving space on passenger ships and other rescue ships to women and children. Just before the holo stations began to go off the air, however, things were getting frantic at the commerical ports, and security guards were trying to keep order. Men had begun to push women and children aside to fight for access to the ships. Then everything went black.''

It was possible, but not probable, that Tippy and his son had tried for ship space at a commercial spaceport. Their home, however, had been less than a mile from the military base. Tippy had been a logical woman. She would have figured the odds, and she would have chosen the military base not only for its larger number of available ships but for the imagined protection of disciplined men. He would probably never know for sure how she had died, but it seemed logical that she had been among those throngs of terrified people who were fired upon by this General Bender's Commando and the police.

"Why is St. Paul important to you?" she asked.

"That is not your concern," he said, throwing words she'd spoken to him back at her.

"I'm tired," she said. "I will go to bed."

He watched her move toward her door. His mind was a roil of emotions. Now, at least, he had one specific target for his hatred. One General Bender. And yet he could not single out one military man and leave others out of consideration. And there was something else, something too coincidental to be believed. He could not credit the idea that someone or some agency was spending time and money to find a man who had stolen a ship's launch. He had been presumed dead. And yet there she was, and she'd been on St. Paul.

"There's an old joke," he said, "about two drunks on an interstellar passenger liner heading from Xanthos to Selbelle."

She turned and stood in her door, looking at him.

"One of the drunks said to the other, isn't this a wonderful age? Here you are on your way to Xanthos and here I am on my way to Selbelle and we meet right here."

"I'm too tired to laugh," she said. "Should I?"

His face hardened. "I'm going to be watching you very closely, *Space Officer* Samira."

"What in the hell do you mean by that?" she flared, but he turned without comment and went into his quarters.

"And we meet right here," he said as he slammed the door.

4

Nema came onto the control bridge an hour before time for change of watch. Her color was better. The med unit was feeding her food supplements and tonics, and she felt fine, except for a bit of residual weakness. She had discarded her habitual one-piece and wore a simply cut two-piece suit, the jacket having a turtleneck that seemed to frame her face and feature its beauty as the glory of a rose is emphasized at the end of a long stem.

"We have over four months to spend together," she said, without preamble. "Perhaps we had better talk."

Tob looked at her blankly.

"Obviously," she said, "my mention of having been at St. Paul during the catastrophe had an effect on you. You said, and I quote, that you were going to be watching me very closely. Why? Have you some connection with St. Paul? Do you think that I've been sent here to spy on you, or to try to get some sort of information out of you?"

Tob continued to study her face, his mind working.

"I'm not asking you to tell me anything. Really, I'm not interested. I have guessed that perhaps you were on St. Paul, and if that is the case, I will not retract any opinion I may have voiced while delirious about the manhood of those who trampled women and children in order to get a place on the ship. If you were one of those, you're the one who has to live with it, not I, and it's no concern of mine."

"I was not on St. Paul," he said, forcing his voice to be neutral.

"Good. Perhaps we won't have to discuss this much more," she said. "Let me tell you, in as few words as possible, how I came to be there. It will be necessary to include some information not directly connected with my coincidental presence there, to show you that I had no choice in the matter. In telling you this, I will be revealing, by inference, some information that will contradict what you know about me. I'm doing this in the interest of, well, peace aboard this ship. I will ask you to keep it confidential."

Tob nodded. "I know that your Z card and duty log are false documents," he said.

"Ah," she said. "It takes one to know one?"

He smiled.

"If you knew, why didn't you tell Madison?"

"I needed this job, too, and there had to be two crewmen."

She mused for a moment. "You wouldn't want to make this easier for me?"

"Let me tell you what's bothering me," he said.

"Here I am on my way to Xanthos and here you are on your way to Selbelle and we meet right here?" she asked. "You were, in some way, affected by the catastrophe on St. Paul. It's more than coincidence that two people with St. Paul connections meet aboard a tug at the end of nowhere?"

Tob was thinking that he'd underestimated the woman's mind. "It does seem rather coincidental, doesn't it?"

"Not when you think about it," she said. "Let's take your two drunks. If they'd been intent on getting away instead of getting to Xanthos or Selbelle, and still had the necessity of earning an existence, would it have been beyond belief to think they would have picked the same remote area of the known galaxy? Let's say they both started from the area of St. Paul. Spread around that sector, in a contour very much like a radio telescope antenna, are the metro areas of the U.P. To reach an outback, they would have had to travel through densely peopled areas, unless they worked toward this area of the rim."

"That still leaves vast areas, thousands of routes," he said.

"Let me tell you how I ended up on Pandaros," she said. She paused. "Damn."

"You don't have to."

"I will need at least three six-month tours to save the money I need," she said. "We were doing well until I mentioned St. Paul. I think, and hope, we can work together. With most men, not even the privacy agreement and the monitors would prevent unpleasantness for me. So I'm doing this in self-interest, even if it doesn't concern you."

"So far I've learned little," he said.

"All right. My father was a point man for a large industrial complex on Zede IV. His job was to find new markets and potential sources of raw materials, and he traveled the rim in this sector. When I was ten, my mother and I started traveling with him. The company furnished him an executive yacht, and since, in many ways, he was a private man and liked being with his family, he taught my mother how to run the ship and as I grew, me as well. That way we could travel, just the three of us, without crew.

"My mother had been in the entertainment business, and one of my father's favorite ways to spend an evening in space was to see her dance and perform. She taught me."

"When you were in coma, I looked for something on your tapes to help keep me awake. I saw a holo of you dancing. You're very good."

"Thank you. My mother taught me well. She said the methods of dancing had been handed down in my father's family for centuries. It was unusual. My father liked for my mother, and me, as I became a teenager, to entertain the local dignitaries on outback planets where he was interested in doing company business. He was a strong man, but basically a gentle, trusting man. He'd been a part of a civilization that had long since almost eradicated violence. He knew there were some dangers outside the U.P.

system, on the isolated outback planets, and he took precautions, but he simply did not have the capacity in him to imagine absolute evil."

She went to the dispenser and drew two cups of coffee, handed one to Tob. She seemed to be having difficulty in continuing.

"I was fifteen when it happened," she said. "We were on a planet called Cerro. It's about ninety degrees arc from here in the plane of the galaxy. It was so remote that U.P. influence was nonexistent. It was a small, cold, barren world with gold, and it was populated by scum. My father wanted to trade them machine tools for gold, we did the usual thing and entertained the local officials. To make a long story short, the man in power on Cerro made his own law, and he wanted me. I began to feel that something was very wrong as my mother and I danced for him. I saw four armed men come into the room and stand in shadows along the wall. But it happened so quickly that—"

"You don't have to tell me this," Tob said.

"They killed my father first. They used long, curving swords, and the man who killed him was so powerful that one blow severed his neck, and his head hit the floor with a loud thud. My mother tried to fight, and she was split from the joint of her neck and shoulder down into her chest. I was taken by the dictator of Cerro. I danced for him and was his for five years."

"I'm sorry," Tob said.

"They would tell you, back in the U.P. areas, that slavery does not exist," she said. "When my first owner tired of me, he sold me to a traveling gold trader who smuggled into U.P. areas. I kept praying that he'd be stopped by an X&A ship, and that I'd be freed. He was stopped, instead, by one of General Evan Bender's ships. I was not free. I became the property of Bender. He took me with him to St. Paul when he was concluding an alliance with that planet, and that's why I was there."

She sipped her coffee and examined Tob's expressionless face.

"So, you see," she said, "it is coincidence, Captain. I am not here to spy on you. I won't ask you to tell me your connection to St. Paul, because I don't care. All I want to do is earn enough money to go back to some civilized world and live in peace."

"You escaped this Bender when he abandoned you on St. Paul?"

"Yes. I was put down on the nearest planet to St. Paul. I'd managed to bring the jewels Bender had decorated me with. I say that because he hadn't actually given them to me as a gift. I was property and the jewels were property and we looked good together. I sold the jewels and headed for anywhere outside of Bender's sphere of influence. I found a man on a mining planet who specialized in forging documents and I became a spaceman. I could get by with it because my father had taught me well, and Bender humored me by allowing me to navigate and operate his ship when we traveled."

"This Bender—"

"He's a mercenary," she said. "He operates here." She indicated a sector of space outward toward the rim from St. Paul. "It's outback there, scattered unaffiliated planets with only a token U.P. presence. One of Bender's more profitable contracts was with X&A. He and his Commando were, thus, a quasi-U.P. force, supposedly a force for law and order. In reality, he would do any job for anyone who had money. He exterminated, for example, the men of a mining company trying to move in on an established firm in the meteorite belt around some planet whose name I have forgotten. He moved his Commando to another planet to police an election in which the men in power had no intention of counting the ballots fairly. He has friends on a hundred outback planets, and he's a powerful man."

"Why didn't you simply head for U.P. core and seek protection?"

"That was my first intention. I discovered, however, that Bender had put out a wanted notice on me. It was official. It had X&A blessings. He'd told them that I was a thief, that I'd stolen millions in jewels from him. It was merely thousands. I need money to get very far away from any area where Bender has influence."

For an unguarded moment, Tob was tempted to tell her why he was aboard a tug at the end of nowhere, to tell her why he, too, had forged identity papers, but the thought of voicing it brought back the pain more severely than he'd felt it in years.

"Thank you," he said. "I'm sorry to have had to put you through this."

"The painful parts happened long ago. The rest of it?" She shrugged. "One becomes accustomed to it." Then she fixed his eyes with her own dark ones. "It is easier to become accustomed to freedom. The next man who tries to make property of me will die, or I will die."

Tob smiled. "I believe. You came close with me. But no problem. If you're well enough, we'll resume our regular schedule."

"I might doze a bit on duty, but I'm all right."

In his bed, after he'd tried to tire his body with a strenuous exercise period, he wondered why Nema Samira, a woman who had been used by men, had escaped and his Tippy had died. And then he turned to a consideration of Bender. Bender had had a financial reason to evacuate his troops. Of all the men in authority on St. Paul, it was easiest to point a finger of guilt at Bender. He had ordered the killing of women and children. Whether or not Tippy and little Aaron had been among those who died, Bender stood out as a target.

Bender fell into the category of men that Tob had been studying. Bender was a leader of men, if only a relatively minor one. But Tob's main intellectual interest was men like President Douglas, an elected official, the kind of man who had helped make St. Paul a decent and pleasant place to live. Why would a man like Douglas desert his post? How could a man who had sworn to serve the people run like a coward?

Finding out what made men like Douglas tick had been his goal, or a part of his goals, for three years. Why hadn't Douglas' weaknesses been recognized? Why, down through man's history, had man elected, or followed, men with fatal flaws? Following the Zede war, a thousand years ago, the surviving Zedeian men of power had been tried and executed for the crime of using planet smashers, but the U.P. had won the war by using—guess what?—weapons that destroyed entire populated planets. What were the answers? How could the race learn and begin to choose leaders who would not, under strain, opportunity, or crisis, crack the veneer of civilization?

But, more importantly, just what the hell was Tob Andrews after? Sometimes he thought he was being unbearably pretentious to think that his studies and his thoughts could have any value in the overall scheme of things. Who did he think he was, some egghead original thinker who would discover new axioms of behavior? And exactly what was Tob Andrews' glorious cause? Was it understanding and contribution to man's welfare he sought, or was it simply revenge?

He had a list. The list contained the names of men he would like to interview, in privacy. The list was not complete. Many men who were on the list had died on St. Paul, and were, thus, forever silenced. Others, such as General Evan Bender, seemed hopelessly beyond his reach.

In spite of his occasional periods of doubt, the thing that kept him going, kept him struggling to master the art of making money, and the thing that had, in his defeat, put him aboard a Mule II on an isolated blink route near the rim of the galaxy . . . was pain. The pain he felt each time he thought of the fear and horror that must have been felt by his pretty, gentle, civilized Tippy and his small son when they realized that they were not going to live was overwhelming. He would ease that pain, he had promised himself, with the pain of others, with the pain and then the death of the men who allowed order to break down, who fought for positions aboard the ships.

And he'd been a dismal failure at that, too. After three years he was still no closer to being in a position to operate on a populated planet, to confront powerful and well-known men.

There had been times when he doubted that he'd ever be man enough to return pain for pain, and at such times death had seemed to be a viable alternative. Always, however, he'd chosen to live, to keep on studying, to keep on planning. Being aboard the *Emily X* was his latest plan. He knew of a shipyard, on a dismal, dirty planet, where, for a few million universal credits the profile of the *Emily* could be altered, her serial numbers erased and reengraved, and some of her storage space converted to weapons bays. The problem was that even when he added the money he'd earn in a six-month tour on *Emily* to the money he had, it still wasn't nearly enough to convert a stolen ship, to equip and provision her, and to do the travel, spending, and bribery that would be necessary even to begin to avenge the deaths of his wife and son. Neither Tob Andrews nor Aaron Delton—for he was both—seemed to have the prerequisite abilities to be an avenger.

He was still in a black mood of hopelessness, brought on, he knew, by hearing Nema's account of the last hours on St. Paul, when he awoke to the sleep alarm, drew his breakfast, dressed, and went onto the bridge to relieve Nema. She looked tired, her eyes sunken. However, there was a glow of life and interest to her face.

"There's something coming toward us at sublight speed, port top quadrant," she said.

Tob walked quickly to scan the detectors. The object was just within detection distance. "If it keeps to a straight line course, it'll pass within ten thousand miles of us," he said.

"Nine thousand four hundred fifty," she said.

"Analyzers sniff anything yet?"

"Still beyond range," she said.

"I'll keep an eye on it and be ready to move if it deviates. Must be an errant piece of space rock."

"Not likely a ship, way off a blink range, moving sublight," she agreed.

"If I were you, I'd skip the exercise period," he said. "Get some rest."

"I think you've talked me into it," she said. "Call me when you find out what that thing is."

"If you like."

For what had been described to him as a boring job, tugging wasn't living up to its reputation. Two ships had passed in the first month, he'd had to nurse an ill woman, and now they were going to have company with the passage of a piece of space debris at relatively close range. He wasn't sure he'd be able to stand all that excitement for the rest of the tour, and then another, and another, before he had even the minimum amount of money needed.

He had a delicious concoction of sinfully sweet things from the food dispenser while he drank coffee and watched the visitor come nearer. At the speed it was traveling, it would be within analyzer range in an hour, and would pass within ten thousand miles just before the end of his watch. He already had educated estimates of size. The visitor was shaped like a potato and was in the area of a hundred feet long. At it greatest thickness it had a diameter of roughly thirty feet. He began to build scenarios in his mind. The shape was roughly that of ancient spacegoing vessels, built when man was still influenced by the physics that demanded rocket design to conform to aerodynamics. He imagined an ancient ship, and calculated her value as a museum piece, even fantasized about the visitor being an alien, and thus immensely valuable. For aside from three races that had somehow gone extinct, leaving some records for space-exploring man, man was still alone in his galaxy. Anything alien would make him a rich man with his captain's share.

It was, however, idle dreaming, and he wasn't even disappointed when the first tentative sniffings of the analyzers said stone and iron, and then iron, iron, iron. It was a space rock, an asteroid, and God only knew how long it had been traveling away from the original cataclysm that had sent it spinning into space. As it came closer Tob practiced his skills with the analyzers and got an idea. The thing weighed much more than it should have weighed, much more than the average asteroid, usually a mixture of stone and some metals. This one, he began to realize, was almost 90 percent metal, mostly iron. Before he woke Nema, he beamed a blink stat to Madison, at Dunking on Pandaros, and asked if there'd be enough value to a few hundred thousand tons of asteroid iron to warrant bringing it home. He hadn't taken time to study the economy of Pandaros. It might be that the planet was so rich in easily mined iron that it wouldn't pay to bring home the asteroid.

Madison's answer caused him to grin. "Snag hundred thousand tons iron soonest," Madison sent. "Deliver at end of tour. Usual share terms."

"What price iron?" Tob sent.

"Iron less than gold," was Madison's cryptic reply.

Tob wakened Nema and she came out zipping up her singlet. He briefed her and she took her place at the console. She would handle the ship while Tob navigated and made the capture. Taking a living ship near enough to a spinning, hurtling piece of iron the size of their visitor would require exact calculations and delicate navigating and handling.

"Iron?" Nema asked as she blinked the *Emily* out past the speeding asteroid, positioned her, used the flux drive to match speed with the hurtling hunk of metal. "Iron?"

"What Madison said makes me think it's worthwhile," he said. "See if you can punch up some info on metals on Pandaros while I measure the exact mass of this baby."

"Iron ores on Pandaros," Nema said, a few minutes later, "are buried deep, and the ore is not rich."

"It's still worth less than gold," Tob said.

"Roughly three times the price of iron in metro areas. Ninety credits a ton for refined iron."

"Hmmm," Tob said. "If this is even close to 90 percent pure, that's not bad. If we can get by with claiming crew initiative; we can claim 50 percent of value."

"We don't have to risk it," she said. "We're not required by space law to do it. Isn't that crew initiative?"

"We'll fight hard for it," he said.

The asteroid had both a tumbling and a rolling motion. And it was moving with an inertial force that would make the slightest bump against *Emily* a serious matter. Tob built a computer model of the asteroid and set the computer working. "All right," he said, "the Century says we should kill the tumble first. It's going to be ticklish, Officer Samira."

"Want to take it?" she asked.

"No. I think I'm faster on the computer than you, and you're every bit as fast as I on the controls."

"While we're working," she said, "call me Nema. Saves time from saying Officer Samira."

"Okay. Ease her out in front and keep the velocities matched exactly."

It was done in two quick operations of the flux drive, one to outpace the asteroid, the other to match speed, with *Emily* no more than a hundred yards from the tumbling juggernaut. Tob ran the approach twice on his computer model to check his figures. "Okay," he said, "punch this into the auto. You're fast, but we'd better let the Century handle it." He gave her the figures and her fingers flew.

"Ready," she said.

"Go auto." He held his breath. There was a slight jar as forward flux thrusters fired, slowing *Emily* ever so slightly. They were watching the spinning, tumbling asteroid on the large screen, and it seemed to loom over them as it drew closer and closer, in one moment presenting its length to them and the next throwing its tons of mass toward them as it tumbled.

Now, now, Tob was thinking, and Nema's lips were closed tightly as the computer fired the rear main flux thrusters in a carefully calculated burst and *Emily* shot away just as the asteroid flung its mass in a tumble to be met by the thrust of the flux.

It took only two more blasts to stop the tumble. Now the asteroid arrowed through blackness presenting its smallest end, with a slight spin around its horizontal axis. Stopping the spin was less dangerous, but more delicate.

Roughly rounded, shaped much like a cigar, the asteroid had no flat surfaces to catch the force of the flux blast, and it took four attempts, with *Emily* drifting along at the asteroid's speed at right angles to it, to stop the spin.

"The rest is easy," Tob said. He gave Nema thrust and direction and *Emily* floated down onto several hundred thousand tons of pleasingly pure iron, engaged her tractor beam, perched atop the asteroid like a smaller bird of prey, and blinked the iron and the ship back to post. Nema parked the asteroid at a safe distance from the ship and the blink route and grinned.

"Well," she said, "it's not a passenger liner, but I won't refuse the check."

"You did a good job," Tob said. "You've earned a cup of coffee."

"I'd rather have about one ounce of your brandy," she said. "This is a celebration."

"You talked me into it," he said, starting to move toward the dispenser, but she rose swiftly and did the chore, handed him his glass, tipped hers to clink against it.

"To the first of many scores," she said.

"To ninety credits a ton," he said, drinking. "Those were universal credits?"

"Whoops," she said. "I didn't notice." She, like Tob, had been doing some multiplication. The asteroid weighed just over 600,000 tons. At 90 percent purity, that was over 500,000 tons of iron at ninety credits a ton and that added up to 450 million credits. If the crew share was figured on the initiative bonus, that was 225 million credits to be split thirty–twenty between herself and the captain.

She rushed to the computer, punched up the material she'd read, shook her head in disgust. "Pandaros credits," she said. "At four Pandaros credits to one universal."

Tob used the computer. "That's sixteen-point-eight for me, eleven-point-two for you."

"Well, for a minute there," she said, with a sigh, "we had it made."

"Hey, that's about six years earnings for a planet's president," Tob said. "Eleven million not enough for you?"

"Not nearly. You?"

It would take the major portion of that to refit *Emily*. "I'm not sure," he said.

"Well, it's a start," she said, "and it was fun. It's nice working with you, Captain."

"Since we're rich, call me Tob," he said, adding quickly. "No invasion of rights of privacy, lady, it's just that I'm used to it."

"I've been thinking about that, Tob," she said, looking at him warily. "It's lonelier out there than I ever imagined. Can we just talk, sometimes?"

"With pleasure," he replied, lifting his glass.

5

During the balance of the tour of duty the two crewmen aboard the *Emily X* did not exactly become intimate, but the relationship relaxed to the point that an occasional meal was shared, Nema joined Tob in the recreation area for competitive games and joint viewing of holo tapes, and Tob discovered that the girl had been exposed to no little education. Her special interest was historical and anthropological. Her private library included all the standard works on Old Earth, and scholarly and technical works on the characteristics of the mutated forms of the race that had evolved on Old Earth after the devastation.

Nema's interests were near enough to Tob's that they spent a lot of time in discussions of the nature of man. Nema's view of the race was even darker than Tob's own. Now and then her contempt for the male of the species would abrade Tob's ego and their discussions would become heated. At such times Nema was overcome with emotion, and she would pace the area—whether they were on the bridge or in the recreation room—her eyes flashing dark fire, her lips curled, voicing harsh analysis of the innate evil of the male. Sometimes her arguments were so simplistic that Tob had to laugh.

"Who starts and fights wars?" she asked. "Who holds at least 80 percent of the positions of power in the galaxy? And why, outside of U.P. space, are there no—or at least very few—male slaves?"

"Nema, the argument is probably as old as man himself," he said.

"Oh, yes. There are hints and indications from the ancient material recovered on Old Earth that women were considered property for more thousands of years than they had so-called equality."

"The hormones your body makes, the endomorphs released by your brain—"

"I don't want to hear that old crap," she said heatedly. "Of course there are physical differences. And you brilliant men have not yet been able to invent anything that is a substitute for this." She ran her hands down her sides and along her hips to indicate that she was speaking of the female body. "So there is basically something sick about the male. He is still animal, still shows the instinctive aggressions that appear in the males of most species of animals. There's an interesting example in the rock lizards of Pandaros. The males are so aggressive that the male population is always less than one-quarter of the female population, and yet the males dominate, hold female slaves, their method of domination being severe lashings of the weaker female with the tail—"

"Nema, female slavery is not widespread."

"It only takes one incident to make it evil," she said.

"Actually, it's the dark side of man that fascinates me," he said. "Have you read that ancient collection of antique writings from Old Earth called the Bible?"

"Yes. Men of that race had many wives."

"And that's all you noticed in the book?"

"If there was a god," she said, "and if he were truly a good god, he wouldn't let bad things happen."

"Ah," he said, "but there are two forces, God and Satan. Satan was cast out of heaven and given dominion over the Earth. Man was given free will, to worship the God of the Earth, the evil one, or to worship the true God, the force of good. If man allied himself with God, he then was more powerful than the force of evil."

"Crap," she said. "The source of most of the galaxy's evil is there, between your legs. The same hormones and other bodily juices that make you male make you power hungry, greedy, callous of the rights of others. Dominance of a planet or a sector is merely an expression of the male instinct to dominate other males in order to get the most property or the most attractive women. Moreover, all men are alike."

"If that were true, do you think that a piece of paper and cameras that record our every movement would prevent me from taking advantage of the fact that I'm alone in deep space with a very beautiful woman?"

"I don't want to step on your toes," she said, moving to stand behind a game table, for in that new relaxed relationship she had taken to wearing a body suit without legs during their exercise period, and the costume showed her tall litheness, her perfect body, to good advantage, "but the sex drive is stronger in some men than in others."

He was male. His life with Tippy had been quite exciting. There was nothing wrong with his sex drive. "No," he said, "I think there is something else in some men. I don't know what to call it. Honor, humanity, loyalty. You see it in some species of birds. On Selbelle, for example, there's a waterfowl that mates only once, and if either male or female dies, the other does not take another mate."

His voice had fallen in volume, and he seemed to have difficulty completing the statement. She realized that, inadvertently, she'd brought up a painful subject.

"Tob, your wife died on St. Paul, didn't she?" she asked.

He rose, turned his back. "She was in St. Paul City."

"Tob, there are good men, and I think you're one of them," she said. But that germ of knowledge about him told her a lot. Knowing that he'd lost his wife on the dying planet was the single most revealing piece of information she'd discovered about him.

"Hey," she said, "sorry I steered the conversation to a painful area."

"Not your fault," he said, turning to face her.

"Friends?"

"Friends," he said.

"Good." She picked up her robe, slipped into it, and turned toward the door. "Sleepy time," she said.

The ship's instruments showed that she stayed in the shower longer than usual. Tob sat slumped in the captain's chair, trying to put his mind in neutral, for the visions of Tippy and his son dying were as vivid and as painful as ever.

He told himself that he should not have allowed the relationship with Nema to become friendly. It complicated matters. It had been simple when she had been cold and distant and antagonistic. Then he'd owed her nothing. Now he understood her more, knew that she, too, had goals, and he'd even come to like her. And she very definitely had no place in his plans. He would not, of course, harm her physically, but she would be hurt, nevertheless.

The tenor of their conversations changed, became more scholarly. They discussed all the theories about why the final devastating war had happened on Old Earth, about why the Zede war happened, why, in the outback, man was still selfishly aggressive and grasping. And the first day she joined him in *Emily's* tiny swimming pool, he learned that he was not yet sexually dead, for the sight of her in her skimpy, two-piece bathing suit was both pain and pleasure to him.

"I still can't get used to the idea of swimming in my drinking water," she said as she surfaced, her long, black hair clinging wetly to her well-shaped head.

"All fluids are purified and reused," he said. "That's what I don't like to think about."

She laughed. She had a beautiful laugh, deep and throaty.

And then he walked into the recreation room one day to see her, in the legless body suit, dancing. At first she didn't know he was there. She had that wild, atonal music turned up loud, and her movements were so graceful, so erotic as she exercised that fantastic muscular control, that he was mesmerized. When she did see him she stopped immediately.

"Don't stop," he said. "You dance so beautifully."

And as she continued he told himself that his interest was in the art form of the dance, not in that beautiful body, not in the dark, sloe-eyed dancer herself.

The last months of the tour made up in inaction for the events of the first few weeks. Neither of them was displeased when it was time to lock *Emily*'s beams onto the iron asteroid and blink back to Pandaros. Tob handled the ship as she lowered through the odoriferous atmosphere and deposited the chunk of space iron on an unused pad at Pandaros Port. They were free. They had not made plans to see each other during their planetside time, but upon landing they had an invitation from Melanie Madison for dinner.

"What do you think?" Tob asked.

"She's a friendly lady," Nema said. "I'll go if you will."

Tob stayed around to watch as men from a Pandaros steel plant measured and tested his asteroid. Their initial calculations were within a few thousand Pandaros credits of being accurate. John Madison was pleased. The tug stations around Pandaros had never showed more then the tiny profit figured into the company bids, and Tob's asteroid was the first salvage made by a tug since Dunking had taken over the Pandaros posts. Madison was still glowing when Tob arrived at his quarters just a few minutes behind Nema to find the Madison's dressed formally for dinner, Melanie Madison bubbling with goodwill and questions about their first tour.

Dinner was excellent. During the first part of it Madison held the floor, telling them how happy he was, that the steel company had already cut a check, and that their shares would be ready within two days. He had added the crew initiative bonus without even consulting the home office.

"Here's to a fair man," Nema said, raising her glass.

"I believe in being fair," Madison said. "No use trying to ignore the fact that finding crews out here is not easy. I hope you two will stay with us for a long time."

"Give me a month with solid earth under my feet and I'll be ready to go," Nema said.

Madison looked at his wife uneasily, cleared his throat. "Well, ah," he said.

"I don't like the sound of that 'well, ah,' " Tob said with a wry grin.

"Well, look," Madison said, after clearing his throat again, "you two seem to have adjusted well. At least you're still speaking to each other."

"We got along all right," Tob said.

"A small problem has developed," Madison admitted.

Tob raised one eyebrow at Nema and waited.

"I believe I explained the system we use out there," Madison said. "We have a rotating tug that covers quite a large area in relief of other tugs. It was supposed to have taken over your post to stay there for your month planetside, but it broke down and now there's no relief."

"I think he's saying he wants us to go back now," Nema said, looking at Tob.

"It would add an extra month's pay, and we'll throw in a full month planetside next rotation so that you'll have two months off with pay," Madison said. "I'm in a real bind, my friends."

"Well, we can't have that," Tob said, pleased really. An extra month's pay would help. He had lost nothing on Pandaros, was more comfortable in space. "Any objections, Officer Samira?"

Nema didn't answer immediately, then she looked at Madison. "Why does Dunking run tours as short as six months?"

"It's company policy," Madison said.

"Yes, but other companies sign on a crew for longer," Nema said. "The *Emily* can carry provisions for years."

"Actually," Melanie Madison said, "I think that most companies that keep crews in space for one year, or as much as three, use married couples." She smiled sweetly at Nema. "John and I knew Pete and Jan Jaynes, for example—the couple who brought back *Rimfire* and discovered a new planet in the process?"

Tob nodded. Everyone in the galaxy had heard of Pete and Jan Jaynes. They'd made the biggest killing ever by a deep-space tug crew.

"I have heard that Pete and Jan, rich as they are now, still take a few weeks every year and go off somewhere in deep space in a small yacht just to be alone," Melanie said. "And we know of several other married couples who seem quite happy staying on tugs for two to three years."

"I don't think it's necessary to be married," Nema said, "but I think Captain Andrews and I would be interested in signing on for a longer tour, if the extra bonus made it worthwhile."

Tob picked up on it quickly. "If the bonus was paid in advance."

"Oh, dear," Melanie said, "I must not play Cupid too well."

Tob flushed. Nema laughed. "That's all right, Mrs. Madison, we know your heart is in the right place. It's just that neither Captain Andrews nor I has any interest in romance."

"I see," Melanie said. "I know it's terribly

nosy of me, but I can't imagine two attractive people, such as you two, alone in space for months and months—'' She halted, went red. "Oh, dear, that's terrible, isn't it?"

Both Tob and Nema laughed. "We're just good space buddies, Mrs. Madison. She beats me at handball, but I can lift more weight than she."

"And I'd been imagining all sorts of romantic things," Melanie said. "Such as a wedding before you go back into space."

"Sorry," Nema said, just a trifle coldly.

"I think, my dear," John Madison said, "that you have thoroughly demolished *that* china shop." He turned to Tob. "Under the circumstances," he said, "I think I can get an okay for a one-year tour, with an appropriate bonus in advance."

"Officer Samira?" Tob asked. Nema nodded.

Thus it was that the *Emily* lifted off three days later, newly provisioned, to return to her post. The crew shares for the iron had been paid, along with the wages and bonus for a six-month tour, plus advance bonus for a one-year tour. Tob had visited a number of banks cashing his checks, so that no one bank would have a record of how much in universal credits he carried aboard *Emily*. The sum was pleasing to Tob, for the bonuses were generous. He estimated that he'd have some operating capital left after having *Emily* altered and armed. He went back into space knowing that he would never see the planet Pandaros again, a bit sorry about the shock and disappointment that John and Melanie Madison would feel, for they had been not only friendly but kind, but ready to, at last, set his grand design into motion.

"Well, the scenery hasn't changed much," Nema said, after *Emily* had reached her post and Tob had blink-stated the word of their arrival to Pandaros. "How about some coffee before you turn in?"

"Sounds good," Tob said. There was, he felt, nothing to be gained in the waiting. The procedure was for *Emily* to make weekly reports to the Dunking officer on Pandaros. By leaving now, he'd have a full week to lose himself and the stolen tug in space, then an unknown number of days while Madison tried to contact the *Emily* before he'd be able to find a ship to send out to the post to find out why *Emily* was silent. During that time he'd be driving the ship hard. He had the route laid out in his mind. It led far out the range astride which *Emily* sat, into the emptiness of space outside the galaxy to intercept the route laid by the X&A ship *Rimfire.* He'd put a quarter of the circumference of the galaxy behind him before zigzagging back among the rim stars toward the dingy little planet where *Emily* would be made unrecognizable.

There were two problems, one minor, the other becoming more and more a concern for his conscience. First, he'd not slept for twenty-four hours, and his flight would require that he be awake for a long period of time. Second, there was Nema. He dreaded telling her, dreaded what she would say, dreaded her anger and disap-

pointment when she found that she was going
to be cast out of *Emily* in the ship's tiny launch.
There would be no real danger for her, for the
launch was a good boat, and perfectly safe, but
he'd have to set her adrift far enough away from
a populated planet to give him his escape time
before she could report.

He would sleep for most of the first watch,
then he would move. Losing twelve hours didn't
please him, but it would accomplish two things,
put him at *Emily*'s controls fully rested, and
give him time to adjust to what he had to do to
Nema. He slept for the full period, found Nema
dozing, heard her brief report of her watch. He
waited tensely as she walked into her quarters,
then he went into action. It would take her about
ten minutes to change and come out for her
exercise period. It took him less than two minutes to get the coder from captain's stores and
change the code on her door, thus effectively
locking her in. The next operation took more
time, and was made possible only by Tob's long
experience with the Century Series of computers. He had to break through no less than five
X&A seals, meddle with the ship's official log,
and make some careful new connections to keep
the ship's computer operational. The end result
of his work, after over an hour, was to have
recorded in the ship's almost indestructible operational recorder, a false reading of a flux generator gone wild, an unlikely event, but one
within the realm of possibility.

Having taken the operational recorder from

its position, he carried it into the ship's shop, burned its case with a torch, battered it with a hammer. Then the recorder went out a lock and went spinning off at an angle from the blink route, broadcasting a beep that would lead a search ship to it. When the tapes in the recorder were examined, they would show that an explosion had totally demolished the *Emily*. Anyone aboard her would be presumed dead. If a total search effort was mounted after discovery of the recorder, its personnel would soon become puzzled at the total lack of any debris, but Tob was betting that a total investigation would not be mounted. *Emily* was, after all, only a Mule II–class tug, and there would have been aboard her only two space bums with no surviving kin to insist on a search and investigation.

Now the trip began. Within hours, *Emily* was light-years away from her post, heading into the emptiness of extragalactic space. There, *Rimfire's* route that circumnavigated the galaxy in blinks of thousands of parsecs would allow Tob to put a lot of distance behind him quickly.

Oddly, Nema had not yet used the ship's communication system to question her locked door, or the fact that *Emily* was making blinks as quickly as the generator charged. There was no mistaking the sliding, queer feeling of a blink, and it was not likely that Nema had fallen asleep in the time it had taken him to lock her in and begin blinking.

During the second charge period, after he'd drained the *Emily's* powerful generator twice in serial jumps, he was nearing that portion of the route from which he would leave the emptiness of intergalactic space and begin to lose *Emily* among the scattered stars of the rim. Within an hour, he would be at the blink beacon where he'd planned to cast Nema adrift in the ship's launch. He pushed buttons and said into the communicator, "Nema, are you awake?"

"I'm awake," she said, her voice giving him no clue to what she was feeling or thinking.

"I want you to pack your things," he said. "You're going into the launch. I'm not going to hurt you in any way."

"How much time?" she asked.

"Just over an hour. I've checked the launch. It's optimum in all systems. It's well provisioned. It'll take you about four days to reach a U.P. planet. There'll be other independent planets nearer, but I'd advise you to get back into the U.P."

"I don't suppose you're going to tell me what you're doing or where you're going?"

"No," he said. "Please be ready. You'll have a lot of questions to answer once you're on a U.P. planet and then you can either go back to Pandaros and work for Madison or send for your money."

"Don't worry about what I'll do," she said.

He closed the communicator and concentrated on his route. When he reached the blink beacon he'd selected, he went to stores, strapped on the ship's saffer, and opened Nema's door. At first he didn't see her. He turned his head. She was wearing a white singlet. She stood to the left of the door, a weapon like his in her hand.

"Tob, I've got the power turned as low as possible on this thing," she said. "And if I have to shoot you, I'll aim below your knees. It won't kill you, but I don't think you'll walk again for a long time."

Her weapon, like his, was a saffer, a standard APSAF, the acronym standing for Antipersonnel Small Arms Fatal. There was supposed to be only one aboard, and that one, the captain's weapon, was strapped to his hip.

"Tob, pull your saffer."

"Why?" he asked.

"I'm not going to shoot you unless you force me to," she said. "I just want to show you that I have discharged your weapon. Take it out and try it."

He pulled the weapon from its holster, aimed it at a wall, pulled the trigger. The saffer was designed for shipboard use, and would not damage metal or electronics. Nothing happened. Nema pointed her weapon to the same wall and a charge ripped, sizzling, through air and sparkled against the wall.

"I followed you on Pandaros," Nema said. "I saw you cash all your checks and bring the money on board. I knew you were up to something, because that was a lot of money, and it would draw a lot of interest during a year's tour."

"Why didn't you tell Madison?" he asked.

"Curiosity, I guess," she said. "You're not going to make me shoot you, are you?"

"Not if I have a choice," he said. "What do you have in mind if you don't have to shoot me?"

"A talk," she said. "Move out onto the bridge and sit in the chair, Tob."

He moved. He moved very carefully. At best, if she fired, he'd have paralyzed legs for months. She came to stand facing him, the weapon expertly trained on him.

"Well?" she asked.

"It's just as I told you. I was going to put you in the launch, here. It would have taken you about four days to reach a U.P. planet, two to reach the nearest inhabited planet. That's all."

"Tob, you didn't give me a choice. You were being a man, making decisions for me. I don't like that."

"So now what?" he asked. "Going to lock me in my quarters and go back?"

"I don't know," she said. "That depends on what you had planned for the *Emily*. Where were you going to have her refitted?" She smiled when he looked up. "You're too smart to try to travel too far in a stolen tug."

"About two day's blinking," he said.

"How do you know you can get her altered without being double-crossed?"

"Just as you know there's slavery in the galaxy, I know there are honest crooks," he said, with a grin.

"Isn't it a marvelous galaxy we live in?" she

asked. "Is the planet of your destination where you got your forged papers?"

"Yes. I spent some time there. Did a couple of illegal runs out of there for the people I'm going to see."

"And then what? You've got several million universal credits. It'll take many to get *Emily* altered. You must have a big score in mind, because you said you've got enough to live well with for a long time, or to start just about any kind of small enterprise. How big, Tob?"

He shrugged.

"Tob, give me a choice. You could have asked me to come in with you, you know. I might have, if the potential rewards are great enough. But you didn't give me a choice. You just assumed that I'd say no and you were going to put me out in space in a tin can. I'm going to do better by you. I'll give you a choice. Tell me your plans and give me a chance to join you or not to join you, or I'll lock you in quarters and blink to the nearest X&A station and turn you in as a pirate."

"What I had planned didn't necessarily mean that I'd become rich," he said. She just stared at him. "There were six men in St. Paul City who might have been able to keep order during the panic," he said. "The president of the planet, the governor of the district, the mayor of the city, the police chief of the city, the fleet admiral for the sector, and the colonel in charge of the St. Paul defense force in the city. You added another name to my list—General Bender."

"Revenge?" she asked. "Is that all?"

"I want to talk with those men first."

She made a face of disgust. "Tob, all this study you've been doing, do you think that qualifies you to go head to head with such men?"

"They took something from me," he said. "I can't get it back, but maybe, I can take something of value from them."

"Their lives?"

"I don't know."

"Tob, you're a fine man," she said, "but you're not cut out for such a plan. You wouldn't have a chance against Evan Bender. He'd gobble you for breakfast."

"There may be more to me than you know," he said.

"Bender is expert in every weapon that exists," she said. "How many men have *you* killed."

"None."

"Bender would kill without hesitation, and with very little information. It wouldn't matter to him. As the old saying goes, he'd shoot first and ask questions later. That's the difference between you and a man like Bender. You'd hesitate, question the morality of killing him. You'd try to talk first, you said so yourself, and you'd be one very dead moralist."

"Would you like to put that weapon away?" he asked.

She tucked the saffer into her belt.

"You can't defeat men like Bender with book knowledge," she said. "Have you ever known a man like those you want to confront?"

"No."

"I have. They're men, just like you on the surface. But they have a different way of thinking. Self is always foremost with them. Others exist only in their own awareness, and are not, actually, real to such men. Bender has killed many, and they were no more real dead than alive to him."

"You'll be out of it," he said. "You won't be blamed in any way for my taking the *Emily*."

She smiled. "Tob, the best way to know a man is to share his bed. A man gets mixed up in bed with a woman. He confuses closeness of body with affinity of spirit, or affection. He reveals himself in ways he doesn't even understand. I can teach you about men who wield power."

"Why would you do that?" he asked.

"I think it would be more informative if you'd ask me why I followed you on Pandaros. Why I bought this saffer and smuggled it on board. Why I was ready for you when you came into my quarters."

"Such questions have occurred to me," he said, with a half smile.

"I told you that Bender had put out a wanted notice on me."

"Yes, you did."

"In his own way, he loved me. I guess because he considered what was his *his*, and hated to lose anything. I know him, you see, and I know that he won't rest until he finds me, and gets his property back."

"Aren't you putting too high a value on your-self?"

"I know that I won't be truly free until Evan Bender is dead," she said.

He looked at her with a musing expression on his face.

"That's why I needed money," she said. "With money you can buy anything. There are men on certain planets who'll travel anywhere, kill any-one, for enough money."

"Are you saying that you want to go with me?" he asked.

"Under certain conditions," she said.

"Such as?"

"You will not risk my life and yours in an attempt to talk with Evan Bender," she said. "With my help we might be able to get close to him. If we can, and it's safe, then you can have your talk before I kill him."

"How many men have you killed?" he asked.

"Only one," she said, her eyes expressionless.

"And the others on my list?" he asked.

"Bender first," she said.

"And then I'll be on my own?"

She shrugged. "Revenge is the most stupid motivation for any action," she said.

"I'm going to get us moving," he said. "We have a couple of days before Madison starts to worry about not hearing from *Emily*."

"The generator is fully charged," she said.

During a recharging period he looked at her, saw that her profile was more proud and more beautiful than he remembered. She had purchased a different perfume on Pandaros, and its delicate scent was very pleasing.

"I don't know if you'll ever be able to get your money off Pandaros," he said.

She smiled. "You always assume that women are less intelligent, don't you? I told you I saw you bring your money on board."

"And yours is aboard, too?"

"I've never trusted banks," she said.

6

Golden Haven was just about the sorriest planet Nema had ever seen, and shamefully misnamed. The planet's G-class sun was a relatively young star, and Golden Haven was correspondingly young. Too small to have gravity enough to hold its atmosphere, it lost precious molecules to space with each passing hour, and each passing day saw more—the amounts measured in relatively minute quantities—of its precious water to be locked into the two thin polar ice caps that gave the planet its most distinctive features as seen from space.

Most of the planet's surface was desert waste. Only in small land areas near the equator was there life, and there nothing more than primitive spores and lichens. Man had come to Golden Haven for its precious metals, and since the planet was so young that it had not gone through the volcanic periods that lift heavy metals from the core to become caught in the cooling rocks near the surface, the first rich discoveries had been very quickly mined out, progress had passed, moving on, and now Golden Haven was a dying planet. Her atmosphere would be leached away into space within a few thousand years. Her water would be locked into ice caps, and even those sparse evidences of man's civilization remaining to her would be forgotten.

Meanwhile, the planet was a supply depot for mining explorations in rich asteroid belts in the system, and the only stop on a blink route that stretched for three thousands parsecs back toward U.P. areas.

Approaching, having been given clearance to land, Tob said, "Nema, we're just about as far in the outback as you can get and still be in the galaxy."

"I would agree," she said.

"The male population is about four times that of the females down there."

"So?"

"So women are in great demand," he said. "No invasion of privacy, but I think it's best that you pretend to be my woman down there."

"I guess it would be in character for me to say I can take care of myself," she said, with a her deep, throaty laugh, "but, okay. Man and wife?"

"No. The papers would put the lie to that. Just my woman. There's a sort of perverse code of honor among outbackers. If a woman belongs to a man and lets others know it, they leave her alone."

"Shall I cling to your arm and smile simperingly?"

"Just stay with me. Call me by my first name. Don't try to outstare any man, and if someone asks you to have a drink, or dance, or do anything, just say, no, thank you."

"Whee," Nema said, making whoopee circles with one finger.

"And we'll sleep in one room," Tob said, swallowing, watching her for reaction.

"Sounds logical."

He breathed easier. "That would be a tip-off, if we took separate rooms. It would say you're available, that I don't really own you."

"Own?" she asked, her eyes going hard.

"Let's not quibble over semantics."

"All right," she said. "One room."

It was long hours before they made it to their room in the one hotel in Golden City. They'd spent the hours talking with a thin, hard-faced man at the refitting shop at the spaceport. Nema had been impressed with the way Tob did business. He could be hard, she saw, and she felt just a bit better after seeing him in action. He had paid 25 percent of the refitting cost in advance. Another 25 would be paid upon completion, and the remaining 50 percent would be transferred from an outbranch of a U.P. bank parsecs away after the refitted ship was safely in space.

Nema would have preferred to stay aboard *Emily*, but that was not possible, for extensive alterations would have to be made inside as well, in order to make it impossible for anyone to recognize the ship as Dunking property.

They had eaten in the hotel dining room, the food basic but well prepared, and she saw that

Tob was a bit uneasy as they rode the lift to their room. She saw why when he opened the door. There was one rather small bed.

"Look, I'm sorry," he said quickly. "It was the only room they had left. I'll take a couple of blankets and sleep on the floor."

"I suppose we could flip a coin for the honor," she said, "but if you're determined to be a martyr—"

"Martyr or gentleman?" he asked, with a grin.

While Nema used the bath, he rummaged in the closet, found two rather threadbare blankets, and spread them in the only available space, directly beside the bed. Nema came out in a robe. "It's cold in here," she said.

"Power is expensive on Golden Haven," he told her. "They cut off the heat in the rooms at nine o'clock. This is an early-to-bed-and-early-to-rise place."

Nema shivered, jumped into the bed, and pulled the blankets up. "At least you'd think they'd have heaters," she said, referring to standard cold-weather blankets equipped with small batteries and heating coils.

"I'll get a couple tomorrow," Tob said. He went into the bath and did his nightly chores. Nema was lying on her side, her robe having been tossed over the end of the bed, her eyes closed. He turned off the lights and removed his outer clothing. He'd never been a man to own nightwear. The floor was very hard, but he was tired. He was soon asleep. He awoke with his teeth chattering and his skin prickling with cold.

The floor under him seemed, through the thin blanket, to be a bed of ice, and he guessed that it was near freezing in the room. He got to his feet in darkness, wrapped both blankets around him, sat in the one chair, shivering. He could see Nema curled up under the blankets on the bed.

"Tob, are you up?" she whispered.

"Yes."

"I'm freezing."

"That seems to be a general condition," he said.

"Can we get some more blankets?"

"I doubt it. This isn't exactly the Xanthos palace. The night clerk is probably sound asleep. I doubt if you'd get any answer at the desk."

"Put your two blankets on the bed and get in," Nema said.

"Look, I can stand this if you can," Tob said.

"For warmth," she said. "Come on, Tob."

He was shivering violently. He spread his blankets on the bed and crawled in, being very careful not to touch her.

"That's a little better," she said. "But I'm still cold." She moved to him. He had his back to her, his legs drawn up. She cupped herself to his back, and he felt the soft, sweet heat of her body. She was wearing something long and silken.

"You could hire out as a furnace," he said, grateful for the warmth.

"You're chilled through," she said. She clung to him tightly, and soon his shivering stopped.

"Okay?" she asked.

"Great," he said. "Thanks."

He slept. He dreamed that he was in bed with Tippy. The force of it soared in him, made him alive as he had not been alive in years, made his blood sing. He could feel her warm woman's body. The contours of it shaped to his hands. Ah, the sweet wonder of it. And she was responding to him, rolling her warm, soft body atop his. She had come to him many times in that sweet never-never land between sleep and wakefulness, and he had come fully awake with the union, to savor her love, to rejoice in her. And it was the same as always, so sweet, until, with a hoarse cry, he knew what he'd done and thrust Nema's body off and away.

"Nema, I'm sorry," he said.

"I know you were more than half asleep."

"I'll get out of bed. I didn't—"

"Tob, it means nothing to me," she said softly, putting her hand on his chest. "But you're a man and you've denied yourself for a long time." Her hand went down to his stomach. He was acres and acres of ache and need and pain and shame for having broken his word to the woman. And yet she was pressing tightly against him, the silken gown pulled high, flesh on his flesh, and then quickly, skilfully, she was on him, and he forgot his pain and his shame as nature's most potent force surged in him. She was wonderfully alive, until, with quickness, it was over for him and she immediately relaxed, kissed his cheek softly, and let her weight lie on him.

"You?" he whispered.

"Don't worry."

"But—"

"I told you it means nothing to me. I do it for you by choice." She laughed that purring, deep-throated laugh. "And there's nothing that raises body temperature better. Warm now?"

"Just right," he said.

She slipped from his arms and lay by his side.

When he awoke the room was beginning to warm with the heat from its two small registers. Nema was dressed, standing in front of the dresser brushing her long, black hair.

"Are you speaking to me this morning?" he asked.

She turned, smiled. "Hi. It's a beautiful morning—for Golden Haven. I'm starved."

"Be with you in a minute," he said, throwing back the covers, then realizing he had on only his underthings.

"Modesty?" she asked as he drew the cover up.

"Nema, about last night—"

"I know," she said. "You were saying your wife's name when you first put your arms around me, Tob. Its all right."

"I swore that I wouldn't invade your privacy."

"You didn't. I gave you entry." She came and sat down on the side of the bed and took his hand. "We're going a long way together. I can't say, never having loved, that I know how you feel about your wife, Tob, but it must be very painful for you. I know that a man has needs.

I'm very good at fulfilling those needs, and for the first time in my life I don't mind. Don't ask me why. I don't know. It's just that I don't mind you having me if you need me. Call it friendship, I guess."

"I won't impose myself on you again," he said. "But thanks."

That day he bought heaters, blankets with batteries and heating coils, and there was no discussion that night. They got into the same bed, and she cuddled close, with her back toward him. Her actions were, he felt, contradictory to her stated feelings, for she seemed to like bodily touch, slept with some part of her in contact with him always, and, at times, with her beautiful, warm, smooth-skinned thigh thrown over his legs, her arm over his chest. Two nights later, as she lay thus, breathing in deep sleep, his needs betrayed him, and he was sleepless for the balance of the night. He was not going to betray his love for his wife again. There seemed to be something vaguely unhealthy about Nema's offer to fulfill his needs, even when the action meant nothing to her. She did not guess, or at least she didn't mention it if she did, that the nights became a moral testing ground for Tob.

One day Tob rented a rugged ground car and they drove into the wastelands, following rutted, wind-eroded mining roads into an arid, cold landscape that seemed to shout loneliness. They walked for a while, Nema collecting and exclaiming over colorful pebbles and rocks. The yellow sun penetrated the murky atmosphere with a hint of warmth, and Tob was reminded of the good days on St. Paul. For the first time his memories of Tippy and his son did not cause pain.

The days took on a sameness. After breakfast in the hotel dining room they would go together to inspect the progress of work on the ship. All markings and the tug's name had been removed immediately. Weapons pods had been added to alter the basic contours of the working vessel, and a totally useless but decorative outer shell had been built over her prow, altering her lines into those of a custom yacht. The owner of the dishonest refitting shop knew his business, and his workmen were skilled.

Changes to the interior of the ship were purely cosmetic, and there Nema participated, choosing colors and decor. The effect was pleasing. The owner of the shop suggested that for a few thousand credits an extra layer of radiation proofing could be included in the outer shell that changed the tug's profile. "Redundant, but cheap," he said. Tob told him to go ahead. In deep space radiation was a minor problem. The galaxy had billions of stars, any one of which emitted enough radiation to break down the finest radiation shields if a ship came near enough to a star's nuclear furnace, but those billions of stars were spread among a roughly circular area over thirty thousand parsecs in diameter, so that in spite of the numbers and sheer mass of stars, emptiness was the rule. Only in those dense star fields toward the center of the galaxy did radiation become a significant factor. Radiation shields protected crew and passengers from that small amount of radiation that penetrated the vast, black spaces between stars, and from the flow of particles from a local sun when the ships were nearing planetfall, but no one ever took a ship near enough to a blazing star to cause problems to a ship's shielding. The additional shielding added to the tug was a safety factor that, Tob felt, he'd never need, but as the man said, it was cheap and it made some use of the outer shell.

Golden City offered little in the way of entertainment. The nightly shows in the hotel's dining room were the only real nightlife, and both Tob and Nema enjoyed them for a few nights, until it became evident that the cast of singers, dancers, and other performers did not change, and that the comedian's material repeated itself every third night.

Nema's beauty, of course, attracted attention, and it wasn't long before they knew all the regulars at the hotel. True to the unwritten code of the outback, men looked, made probes of investigation of the new and beautiful woman, but observed the code when Nema politely refused their attentions.

A few excursions into the arctic wastelands exhausted their interest in the outdoors, for there was a sameness there, and a lack of life, that made such outings vaguely melancholy. A solution to their boredom came as it were, by an evolutionary process. They tended to hang around the shop, watching the men at work on their ship, and little by little became a part of the working crew. It beat hanging around the hotel. Both of them worked hard and by the time they were ready for bed they were both tired. So it was that Tob's disturbing awareness of the woman in his bed was sublimated into his physical exertion and resulting tiredness.

Three months after their landing on Golden Haven, the work was nearing completion. "We need a name for her," Tob said one day as the workmen applied the final coat of bonded paint.

"I've been thinking about that," Nema said. "I think it would be nice to name it after your wife."

He shook his head.

"Why not?" she asked. "Because of what happened the first night in the hotel?"

"No," he said. "It's just that—" He looked at her. "For a woman who demanded a contract to protect her privacy you can be damned nosy."

She laughed.

"Tippy hated violence," he said. "I don't think she'd approve of what I want to do. She wouldn't want her name associated with such a venture."

"Then name it after me," Nema said, with a hard glare.

"I've been toying with that idea," he said. "But indirectly. I've been thinking of calling her *Dancer*."

Dancer she became. She was finished, and with yard engineers aboard, she fluxed up into space and both Tob and Nema had lessons in weapons operation. The old *Emily* had become a deadly vehicle. One of the engineers said, "In capable hands, she's the match for a fleet destroyer."

"I want to work with you until I meet that definition," Tob said.

"Well, you're pretty good already. The little lady is a bit faster with the range finder, but you're coming along."

Nema was, indeed, fast. With the helmet in place over her dark hair, her mind directing the weapons systems, *Dancer* demolished a few drifting pieces of space rock, blinked in and out in random maneuvers designed to throw off the fire control of an enemy, and passed all her tests in good order.

"Let the little lady operate fire control," the engineer who was training them said. "You stick to control. You can make a computer talk, and you're better than she at the console, but you can work for a year and she'll still be faster than you at fire control."

When *Dancer* lifted off Golden Haven for the last time, she was watched by the thin-faced man who owned the yard. One blink away, in a direction toward the galactic center, Tob sent a blink stat that released the remaining money owed to the yard, and then contacted the yard with a message that it had been done.

A blink stat came back immediately. "Money transferred," it read. "Remove and jettison orange package in generator cooling vent B-5."

"They play for keeps," Tob said, when he had recovered an explosive device from the cooling vent. It went into space quickly, and Nema set it off with a laser. "He was going to get his money or else."

"We should have anticipated something like that," Nema said, her face showing concern. "He was in control. That's the type of world we're going to be operating in from now on, Tob. We've got to anticipate. We've got to learn to think like them."

"I think, just for the heck of it," Tob said, "that I'm going to give this ship a once-over."

He began on the bridge, and it was a time-consuming process. After he'd made certain that there'd been no tampering with the computer, he could use it to check areas of the ship, such as the interior of the blink-generator chamber, that were inaccessible to him. The search took him four days, during which he slept only for a few hours at a time. Nema was taking the ship back out toward the rim in the meantime.

He found the transmitter in the outer tube of the flux drive. He'd donned space gear and had crawled every inch of *Dancer*'s hull, poked into every indention, used instruments to look inside the false prow. He brought the transmitter into the ship with him, after he'd determined with a sniffer that there were no explosives inside it.

"I wonder why this?" he asked. "It's transmitting continuously, but the signal travels at light speed. They couldn't locate us unless they were within a few thousand miles."

"Just insurance," she said. "They always want

to have an ace in the hole, even if it gives them just a tiny bit of an edge."

"Let's go over it again," Tob said, not liking the idea that somewhere else on the ship might be some kind of device. It didn't make sense. What could the yard owner have had in mind? Just playing the angles? Making it possible to locate *Dancer* just in case, at some time in the future, it would be an advantage? He himself would never have thought to take such measures without any immediate use for them in mind. That form of constant competitive warfare among men was not a part of him, and he mused over it for a long time as both he and Nema went over the ship in minute detail. Would he have a chance against such men, men who were always on the alert, who were always scheming, always looking for an advantage?

When Nema accompanied him in an outside inspection of the hull, it was the first time she'd ever been in space gear and outside the protective, deceptively secure hull of a ship. Looming over the prow of *Dancer* was the disk of the galaxy, a silvered glory. Seeing it from the outer fringes of the Perseus arm, they could get a faint idea of the galactic contour, the band of dense stars bulging at the center, and the sight froze Nema for a long minute.

"How beautiful," she whispered. "How very beautiful."

"The U.P. metro areas are in that direction," Tob said. "Old Earth is off to our right, in the Orion arm. We'll be headed there." He pointed toward the right end of the sweep of disk stars. "We'll hit *Rimfire*'s route and swing down the Vulpecula range."

When, after several more days, they were certain that *Dancer* held no more surprises for them, they slept while *Dancer*'s generator recharged, had a pleasant meal together, topped off the meal with a glass of fine brandy. By unspoken agreement, they had abandoned the twelve-on-twelve-off watches. Their lives had, somehow, become timeless, and although there was a purpose, a goal, there seemed to be no pressure. Each slept in his own quarters, leaving the ship's sensors and monitors to stand watch as *Dancer* lay motionless in space. During recharge periods they played games and exercised, swam, watched holos together, worked as a team while the ship was covering the parsecs-long blinks.

There came a time, however, when they had to speak of their plans. It was Nema who brought up the subject. "We can send a blink stat ahead to an X&A station and ask for the present whereabouts of Bender," she said over a meal of fine Pandaros steak.

"Blink stats cost money," he said. "And we have no established line of credit in *Dancer*'s name."

"We could use the Dunking company credit code."

"Too risky," he said. "We'll be in the Vulpecula sector in a few days. We can make planetfall and do some checking in a library. There's a planet a few parsecs from St. Paul that is a U.P.

protectorate. It's civilized. I want to check to see if my information on ex-President Douglas is still current. We should have no problem locating a man of Bender's stature."

"You're in no hurry, are you?"

"Are you?"

She shrugged. "Tob, while I was running, making my plans for the future, I began to make a collection of tapes of planets on which I might like to settle. Care to see some of them?"

"Sure," he said.

"I'm not particularly interested in living on a metro planet," she said. "I've spent my life among the rim worlds. I've seen holos of places like Xanthos, and life would be just a little too frantic for me there. What I have thought about is a planet with minimum-protectorate status, so that there'll be U.P. law and order, but not too crowded. Then there's the money angle, too. Money goes a lot further on an outworld. Land is cheap, and you can live well on less than half of what it would take to live on a metro planet. I'd like a place where there's some cultural activity, though."

"Pretty tough combination, cheap rent and high culture," he said.

"There are such planets." She punched up a tape and they watched scenes of life in pleasant cities with wide, well-shaded avenues, saw landscapes of beauty. "This one," she said, "is my favorite, so far. It's on the far end of the Orion arm, toward the southern cross. It's mainly an agricultural world."

Broad plains rippled in cereal crops. Towering mountains offered fine ski slopes. There were tropic seas and islands thick with broad, flat-leaved, fruit-bearing trees.

"They have a planetary dance group that is so good it tours into U.P. central worlds," she said.

"Ambitions?"

"Oh, no." She laughed. "I'm afraid that my talents are limited. Once I do my so-called ancient dance I'm finished. They have immigration restrictions. To settle there you have to show a pretty solid net worth. With what we have now we'd just pass the requirements. And we could put *Dancer* out to charter to earn more money."

She'd been talking in a soft, dreamy voice.

"I'd want to live in the foothills of the main range of mountains on the southern continent," she said. "I like a place with a definite change of seasons. I stayed in a ski lodge once, on some world I don't even remember, with my mother and father, and we had a wood fire in a huge, stone fireplace. I can still remember how pleasant the heat of an open fire was, how cozy it was with snow outside."

"Nema, if you want out, I'll drop you off," he said.

She was silent for a long time. "Tob, I've learned something about myself in the past months."

"Want me to ask what?" he said, when she was, again, silent for a long time.

"I've been essentially alone since my parents

were killed," she said, "even if I was always being told what to do by a man. I've had plenty of time to get to know myself." She laughed. "I've heard you snicker, and make little remarks, when the characters in some holodrama revealed confused and deep motivations for their actions. Remember that interplanetary spy story we watched just a week or so ago, when the main character was so deep and so complicated that we both laughed? And I've heard you say that you feel that psychoanalysis is an ancient farce. I think I'm too simplistic to be complicated. I never seem to be confused, and I've never had to fight great battles within myself. It's not that I'm always sure what I'm doing, it's just that things always seem to be black or white with me, no complicated shades or blends of colors."

"I think I understand," Tob said.

"I was asking myself why I came with you," she said.

"What did you answer?"

"That I suppose I'm still a bit immature."

"I'm not sure that's complimentary," he said.

"Not you, me. Tob, I came within a inch of leaving when it became apparent that you had some plan that in all probability did not include working another full tour for Dunking Deep Space Limited. And it terrified me. I realized that I'd been terrified all the time I was on my own after ridding myself of Bender. Since childhood I've always had a man directing my life. First it was my father, and then the others. I told myself, Nema, you're a big girl now. You're free. And it scared the living daylights out of me. In short, I came with you not so much to have my revenge, and to make myself safe from Bender, but because I didn't feel secure, or confident enough in myself, to make my way without the guidance of a man."

"That's a heavy load," Tob said musingly. "I don't know if I'm capable of living up to it."

"Or is it that you just don't want the responsibility?"

"I look on us as working partners, who happen to be male and female," he said.

She smiled. "And that, perhaps, is why I'm here. You treat me as an equal. You make no demands, but you showed me on Golden Haven that you have the natural appetites of a man. I won't bring this up again, but I will say, Tob, that whatever you need from me is yours, with no obligation."

He was watching the play of reflected light in her large, dark eyes. "I guess I'm a simple person, too," he said. "I know it's not exactly normal to still be carrying a torch for a woman who's been dead for years. But she was a part of me. She was my life. I keep thinking of that bird I mentioned once, the species that mates for life, and does not remate even if his mate is killed. Maybe that's not so simple, but that's the way it is." He held up his hand as Nema started to break in.

"I like looking at you. You have the most beautiful body I've ever seen. I like the way your mind works. You're easy to be with." He laughed. "Once we ironed out the kinks. I love watching you dance. But I don't need to feed my male appetite, Nema. I've never been able to separate that aspect of male-female relationships from love, and without love it isn't even efficient exercise."

She laughed delightedly, then sobered. "That I'm sorry I have missed. I'm sorry that I will never be able to experience love."

"And so, we're friends," he said. "But you're beginning to have doubts? The offer to drop you off on your little paradise planet is still open."

"You're going ahead with it?"

He nodded.

"All right," she said. "There's something you have to see."

He looked, interested, as she rose, punched a code of access to her private library. "I took these from the captain's records on the last ship to leave St. Paul City," she said. "I'm showing it to you because you're just not hard enough. To do what you want to do you're going to have to hate more."

He steeled himself, suspecting what he was going to see. He saw a scene of pandemonium. The holo image showed an area of landing pads, then zoomed to the far fences to show hoards of people, people who screamed, fought, begged, wept. He saw men climb the backs of women and other men, lashing out with feet, fists, weapons in an effort to reach the fence. He saw squads of men in combat armor dogtrot toward the fence, saw the blaze and heard the crackle of weapons, the screams of pain as people died outside the fence.

He could hardly breathe. He scanned the rows of faces, ever-changing faces, panicked faces, dying faces, both hoping for and praying against seeing the face of Tippy. He saw the fences give way before the throngs pushing dead bodies forward. He saw armored soldiers kill hundreds, fall back. He saw the angle of the holo camera lift and knew that the scene was being filmed from a rising ship, saw the mob rush a ship on the ground and saw it swarmed under and then he heard the crashing, thundering, wind-tortured death of a world.

He could not move. The image in the holospace had faded.

"Can you still blame one man, or several men, for that?" Nema asked.

He had not, of course, seen Tippy in the doomed crowds. At least he'd been spared that.

Nema punched up another tape. "This is Evan Bender," she said.

Bender was in uniform. He was a tall man, around six-six, Tob estimated. He was muscular and young and his sneer of cold command made him handsome, in a distant sort of way.

"This is a record of an official visit to an outplanet where he hoped to get a contract for furnishing security troops," Nema said as Bender was shown bowing and shaking hands with a paunchy, older man in a colorful, fanciful uniform. Then the scene switched to a banquet table piled high with delicacies. Bender sat next to the man in the colorful uniform.

"The rest of it is a record of negotiations," Nema said, turning off the holo. "But that's Bender. Still want to confront him?"

"I still haven't figured out how," Tob said.

"I can get him to come to me," she said. "Can you, then, kill him, in cold blood, without giving him a chance to kill you?"

"I want to talk to him."

"Tob, face it. There'll be no talking. If you get one chance to kill him, that's it. He won't be lured into a trap twice. You're going to have to make up your mind. What do you want to do, hear Bender say he couldn't stop the events on St. Paul?"

"I just want to know why something wasn't done."

"Because, damn it, he's human, just as all the others in charge were human."

"But you could get him to meet you, alone?"

"Yes," she said, "if you're sure that's what you want."

"You want to be free of him, once and for all, don't you?"

She took a while to answer. "Yes." She rose. They were in the recreation room. She touched the light panel, gave color to the illumination, slid out of her white coverall singlet. She wore a simple, decorative bra and pantlets with lace. Music began, and in the pulsing, colored lights she danced. She danced with an abandon that he had not seen previously, and the dance became more and more frantic, energetic, until, in a wild crescendo, she finished, legs split, head bowed, dark hair hanging in front of her face. When she looked up there were tears in her eyes.

Tob's chest was constricted from the sheer beauty of the dance. He could not speak. Nema rose, pulled on her singlet, and left the room. Tob went to the bridge and blinked *Dancer* closer to her destination.

7

Nema came out of the dressing room of an exclusive women's shop on the planet Norma and examined herself in a full-length mirror. She turned to face Tob. She wore a simple, classic business suit, and she wore it exceedingly well.

"Very becoming," said the saleslady. She turned to Tob. "It's made for your wife," she said.

"Yes," Tob said. "I like it."

"My dear," the saleslady said, "we have just received a shipment of evening wear from Tyros. It's as if the entire collection has been designed for you."

"We won't be needing evening wear," Tob said.

Nema's face fell. She'd been looking like a small child in a candy shop until then.

"But let's see it," Tob said quickly, and Nema gave him a blazing smile. He didn't quite understand. She was spending her own money, and yet she was reluctant to make even one decision without his approval. At first, as they had begun to shop, to prepare themselves for life on a civilized planet, he'd been a bit uncomfortable. But it was nice to see her in various costumes. He saw other women in the stores, some dumpy, some too thin, and he couldn't help but be flattered a bit when Nema got the immediate attention of the salespeople and the envious stares of other customers.

Nema in a silver creation that showed her shoulders and tantalizing, smooth skin in décolleté, brought a gasp of admiration from the saleslady and a grin of appreciation from Tob. "Take it," he said. "We'll start dressing for dinner aboard ship."

"Oh, that was fun," Nema said later as they taxied back to their hotel. "I haven't done that in years and years."

"Better make it more years or you'll be broke," Tob said.

"Don't be a killjoy," she said.

In the room she had to model each purchase again for him, and he found himself laughing with her in her pleasure. She wore the silver creation at dinner in the hotel dining room. Tob was rather handsome, he had to admit, in black-and-white evening wear. In his arms, as they danced to a synthesized waltz, she was giggly and girlish. It was a side of her that he had not seen, and he was fascinated.

Their relationship had become more casual over the months and weeks, especially after sleeping together for warmth on Golden Haven. Back in the room she carefully removed the silver gown, hung it, and danced around the suite in new and quite daring lingerie, still feeling the spell of the music, the night, the pleasure in being back among civilized people. Tob was less casual. He still did not feel comfortable mostly nude in front of her, and covered himself with a robe as he did his nightly toilet and prepared for bed. She, having finished ahead of him in her own bath, sat on her bed dressed in a frilly little nightgown, legs crossed.

"Tob, let's get on with it, get it over. I liked today and tonight. I want more of it."

During the day Tob had done some research, mostly by vidcon, with the city library. "Douglas is still here," he said. "His estate is about three hours out of the city by groundcar."

"Well, that's a good idea, taking an easy one first," she said. "Tomorrow?"

"Yes. I called. We have an appointment. We're from the University of Golden Haven. We're making an in-depth study of the reactions of people involved in potentially fatal crisis. Douglas said he'd be happy to cooperate."

"I didn't know there was a University of Golden Haven," she said with a smile. "I didn't know anyone on Golden Haven could even read."

"Well, there is now, at least as far as Douglas is concerned. We'll move *Dancer* to a small, commercial field twenty miles from the estate. You'll stay with the ship."

"No," she said.

"Nema—"

"Look, it's my neck, too. If you do something

stupid and get caught, they'll come after me. I'm going with you."

Tob made a face, but fell silent. Nema lay back, flinging her arms out. The room was pleasantly warm and she was not under the cover. The short gown showed a nice length of legs. "The bed feels so good," she said. And, within minutes, she was asleep. Tob wished that he could be so casual. He did not know what would happen next day when he saw Douglas. He was prepared for anything. Even on a civilized planet, a man who knows his way around can find and buy almost anything, and he had, in his case, a deadly little projectile weapon that fired in absolute silence, sent an explosive, tiny pellet to a target at short range and was guaranteed to be fatal in contact with any portion of a human body.

The relatively crowded airways of the planet Norma made for some careful flying on flux. They had to wait in orbit before getting landing clearance at the small commerical field, but a rental groundcar was waiting for them, and the drive to the estate of ex-President Douglas of St. Paul took only a half hour. Douglas' manservant admitted them to a palatial salon on the ground floor of a very impressive mansion.

"Mr. Douglas will be with you in a few moments," the man said, leaving them.

"He did well for himself," Tob said.

Nema put a finger to her lips. "Ears and eyes," she whispered.

Morton Douglas entered the room in a self-propelled wheel chair. He had aged severely in the years since the destruction of St. Paul. Tob would have had trouble recognizing him, although he'd seen Douglas on holo many times.

Nema, wearing the neat, simple little business suit, stood first and Tob followed suit.

"At least my eyes will be nicely entertained as I am questioned about a terrible tragedy," Douglas said as he kissed Nema's hand.

"Ah, you politicians," Nema said, "always so good with words."

"Sit down, sit down," Douglas said. "I must ask that we get down to business immediately. My stamina is not what it used to be, you know."

"President Douglas," Tob said, "almost one billion people died on St. Paul. It is mankind's worst disaster. We have, of course, read your own book on the subject, and we also have an extensive file of the various interviews and articles which contain statements from you regarding the tragedy. We have, actually, only a few questions that we feel have not been adequately covered in previous material, and I'm afraid, sir, that some of them might seem, on the surface, to be insulting. We ask for your patience in the interest of science."

"The study of people can never be a science," Douglas said.

Nema laughed lightly.

"You have stated many times, sir," Tob said, "that you felt you could be of value alive, that you left the planet in order to have the nucleus of a government surviving."

"Yes, that's true," Douglas said.

"The question is this, and it's a blunt one. How could you possibly believe there'd be anything to govern once the planet turned on its axis? Didn't you know that there'd be total destruction? I'm sure you're aware that you have been criticized for having saved your own skin while women and children died for lack of space on the ships."

"I take it, young man," Douglas said, "that you have not had access to the book by Bader and Clark?"

Tob looked at Nema. They'd just reviewed the Douglas material a few nights previously, as they approached Norma. "No," he said.

"Well, it's relatively new, and since the disaster is now years old, there's not as much interest in it as there once was. Bader and Clark made use of classified material from my personal files, material that was just declassified last year. I'll brief it for you, and I can give you a copy of the book when we've finished here. I had quite conflicting advice in the last days of the planet. There was a U.P. scientific team on the planet. Among our own scientists we had severe extremes of opinion. On the day of the disaster, for example, our most respected scientist went on the holo to pooh-pooh the disaster criers. He said St. Paul was as stable as any planet, that there were many other planets that had developed polar wobbles much more severe than that of St. Paul's. On the other hand, there were the Cassandras, but they had cried wolf so often very few listened to them. They'd been predicting disaster for two centuries, with exact dates of the cataclysms given by some new voice of doom once a month.

"I had asked for a commission of scientists from the U.P. to winnow out the truth from the conflicting opinions. They were government employees, and you know civil servants, reluctant to make definitive statements. Their original report to me was simply a rehash of opinions given by scientists over the decades. They came to no conclusion one way or the other. They were at the north pole of St. Paul when the planet turned."

"You were a popular and respected president," Tob said. "If you had stayed on the planet, instead of leaving, what could you have done to prevent the riots? Could you have kept calm, and allowed women and children first place on the evacuation ships?"

"I've asked myself that question a million times," the old man said. "I still don't know the answer. Perhaps, if I had been there, I could have kept the peace a bit longer. If I had been there, however, I'm not sure I would have insisted that space be allotted to woman and children first."

"Why?" Tob asked, rather stiffly.

"There was a a body of opinion among wellrespected men that the disaster would not be total. Many thought that the shift would be a minor one. They had impressive figures to prove that the imbalance would be corrected with a shift of poles not more than 10 percent. In that case, there would have been terrible destruction, earthquakes, floods, storms, but there would have been survivors. Some things would have been salvageable. Life would have gone on. In that event, we would have needed people—regardless of sex—who could minister to the injured, who could rebuild our cities, rescue the stranded, put the planet back in business again. A random selection of women and children would not have accomplished that."

Douglas drew himself up, his face going pale, as if he were in pain. "I think, young man, that I would have done all within my power to ensure the survival of the greatest number of people. I left orders with my people to do just that, to select those who went onto the ships for their skills and their knowledge. It was a terrible decision to make. And yet, why is the life of a woman, or a child, more valuable than the life of a man?"

"Did you leave your wife on St. Paul?" Tob asked, his voice grating.

"Yes," Douglas said, "but in her grave. She had been dead for a number of years. I left two daughters and five grandchildren on St. Paul." He rubbed his left cheek with the palm of his hand. "I often wish that I had stayed. Do you know the Bible, young man?"

"Not thoroughly," Tob said.

"In Genesis, Chapter 6, Verse 3, there is a promise from God. The life span of man shall be a hundred and twenty years. Isn't it odd that on civilized planets the average life span of men is exactly that, slightly more for women?"

"I'd never thought of it," Tob said.

"A promise that, with the help of medical science, God has made come true. But it's not a promise to me. It's a curse."

"A curse?" Nema asked.

"Of that billion people who died, well over 60 percent voted for me in the last election," Douglas said. "Not a day went by that I didn't get thousands of messages wishing me well, thanking me for one of my policies. I think a people, a world, loved me, or at least respected me. That was my world. I was born there and I grew up there. I spent exactly two years off St. Paul in my lifetime, on a tour of the inner U.P. I loved my world and I deserted it. At the time it seemed the logical and proper thing to do. But I wish, devoutly, that I had been there to die with those who loved me."

Tob felt cynicism. "You've done very well for yourself, Mr. President. You're living well."

Douglas smiled sadly. "Yes, that's been said before, too. Did you know that we took the gold in St. Paul's treasury off?"

"I didn't know for sure. There are rumors, reports in certain material."

"And that gold has been distributed to survivors. It was used to give them a start on other planets. It was divided equally among all the survivors. I forfeited my share. I have my U.P. pension. This house I live in is U.P. property. Yes, I live well. My biggest expenses are medical. I use any surplus to maintain a St. Paul museum that stands just a few miles from here. My wife had business interests on various planets before she died, and they've done rather well under the management of the same financial institution that managed them for her while I was in office. Those holdings will go to the museum when I die."

"If you had to name names," Tob said, "the names of the men most responsible for not operating the evacuation more efficiently, the names of men who fired on civilians, who allowed the chaos that made the end even more painful, what names would you choose?"

"The list would be very long," Douglas said.

"Start at the top," Tob said.

"Mayor Landings of St. Paul City panicked," Douglas said. "That's well documented. He didn't follow my orders. Instead, he usurped a ship for his own family and the ship left only partially loaded. Chief of Police James Toll died trying to enforce order, on the other hand. District Governor Donald Watkins sold space on his private yacht, one berth cost ten million universal credits. It was not a crime. It was his yacht. Fleet Admiral Flehow, I have been told, ordered his men to fire on civilians who were disrupting the orderly evacuation at the naval base."

Tob waited.

"But blame? I blame myself for being alive. I have watched the last holos from St. Paul City. I can blame every man, every woman, who became a part of that mob. But, in the end, what did it matter? They were all dead, and they knew it. It would have been nice if they had died with human dignity, but haven't you ever seen a dying man struggle against death? He tenses his muscles, if he has the strength. He throws his head from side to side. He may, in his struggle, strain so hard that his stomach evacuates itself, and he may lose control of his bowels in his fight. They were dying, and they were fighting against it. I wonder if it wouldn't have been the same on any planet, or in circumstances where the numbers involved were less. The human mind wants to survive, and I have become convinced that it will influence actions that seem shameful to us. Oh, you can counter that with examples of individual heroism, where a man gives his life for others, but that's not the same. On St. Paul, everyone was dead, and everyone knew it."

Douglas was quite pale. His hands had started to shake.

"Any further questions?" he asked, his voice cracking in weakness.

"I came here to kill you," Tob said calmly.

"Ah," Douglas said. "Who did you lose on St. Paul?"

"My wife. My son."

"And how are you going to kill me? I do hope that it won't be too painful." Douglas tried to stop the shaking of his hands by clasping them together.

Tob showed his little projectile weapon.

"Ah, yes," Douglas said. "Good choice. And

humane. The explosive force ruptures cells. The brain is dead before pain signals can be received." He pulled himself up in the chair. "I'm ready."

Tob put the weapon away, stood.

"Please," Douglas said. "Consider it a favor. If you'll call my man, I will give instructions for him not to sound an alarm. You must have plans for getting away. You'll have plenty of time. And it will solve all my problems.

"Please," Douglas cried out, as Tob seized Nema's arm and hurried her toward the front door. "Please don't leave me like this."

In the groundcar Tob was stonily silent for a long time, then he pounded the wheel with the butt of his hand. "Damn, damn, damn," he said.

"He didn't mention Bender," Nema said.

"He left his daughters and his grandchildren to face *that*," Tob said.

"Why didn't you kill him?" Nema asked.

"I don't know. I don't know." He sighed. "Because, damn it, he was as much a victim as anyone."

They slept aboard *Dancer* that night. Tob retired almost immediately. Nema, remembering the desperation in Douglas' voice as he begged to die, could not sleep. She went into the recreation room, drove herself through exercise until her leotards were soaked with sweat, showered, swam, and started back toward her quarters with only a towel wrapped around her. As she passed through the bridge she heard a hoarse, pained, male scream from Tob's quarters, ran to this door, opened it. He was tossing on his bed, the covers twisted around him. He moved to stand beside the bed as he groaned, flailed out with an arm, moaned and cried out his wife's name. Nema, her heart hurting for him, lay beside him, stroked his forehead.

"Hey, Tob, it's all right. Hey, you're having a nightmare."

His eyes opened wide, looked around wildly. Then his arms came up and pulled her to him, the towel falling. He clasped her tightly, flesh on flesh, then, with a sigh, he pushed her away.

"Thanks," he said. "That was a bad one."

"Tob, the life span of man shall be one hundred and twenty years," she said softly, sitting on the side of the bed. "That's a long time to go on punishing yourself like this. What's it going to take?"

"Bender," he said. "One life, one blow. Then I'll quit."

"Bender," she said. "All right. Want me to stay with you?"

"Thanks, but no," he said.

It was not difficult to learn the whereabouts of General Evan Bender. The city library found it for them in minutes. Bender had signed a contract with the Department of Exploration and Alien Search to police the initial settlement and early development of a newly discovered water planet in the Sagitta sector of the rim. That was almost half way around the plane of the galaxy. *Dancer*, freshly provisioned, carrying the luxuries of a U.P. planet in her store-rooms, lifted off and headed for the rim in a series of blinks along well-traveled routes, reached the big blackness of space far past the last rim stars in Scorpius, and turned left. There still seemed to be no sense of urgency but Nema suggested that they work individual watches to speed the trip.

"It's time we ended it," she told Tob. "I want to find my little retreat. I want a place with a clear, cold stream running directly under my bedroom window so that in the mornings I can step out onto a deck and leap into the stream. I won't ever take a shower again, just bathe in my private stream."

Space routine seemed to suit both of them. It was a long, involved trip. In the sector between the Centaurus and Sagitta points of reference, stars were thinly scattered, the area not well traveled. Blink routes, at times, seemed to double back on themselves. They ate well, were entertained well with the new holos that had been purchased on Norma, talked together, sometimes, through one half of the other's watch, exchanged likes and dislikes, told of childhood experiences. And for the first time Tob could talk about Tippy and little Aaron. He could tell of Aaron's joy when his father came home from space without weeping, and with a smile of pleasant memory on his face. And Nema danced for him. He did not even have to ask. She would spend days working on a new routine and then call him into the recreation room, and he'd slump into a chair and watch with great admiration. Never had he seen such a perfect female body.

After months in space, they made planetfall on a world with two weak, pink suns, and laughed together at their double shadows. It was an outback world, and the hotel had large beds, but only one to a room. There were no awkward moments. They ate, showered, retired, and Nema immediately made bodily contact, turning her back to him spoon fashion and settling in with a contented little sigh. He threw his arm over her waist for comfort. There was no desire in him, only a knowledge of that perfect body next to his. He saw her, in his mind's eye, in the various graceful and beautiful positions of the dance, and had an urge to feel the strength of her thigh muscles, the perfect little roundness of her rump. She sighed, turned to face him.

"Tob?"

"Sorry," he said. "I was just thinking about how you look while you're dancing. Just appreciation, lady, that's all."

"Feel free," she said, snuggling to him. He let his hands run down her back, felt the indentation of her spine, the outthrust of her hips.

"It's a rather odd relationship, isn't it?" he asked.

"Ummm," she said.

"It's as if when I'm touching you with my hands I'm participating in the dance," he said.

"I don't mind, Tob."

He removed his hands, turned his back to her.

She sensed his rejection of her, his stiffness. "Well, what the hell do you expect?" she asked. "I am willing to give all I have. If that's not enough for you, to hell with you."

And it suddenly came to him that she had her own ghosts, that he was not the only one who had been damaged. He turned, gathered her into his arms. Her back was, at first, stiff.

"I'm sorry," he said. "I've been thinking only of myself. The ironic part of it is that if you offered yourself to me with love, Nema, I'd still be incomplete, and I'd still hold back."

"I like touching you," she whispered.

"And I like touching you," he said.

"I'm not greedy, Tob. That's enough for me."

He held her until her breathing became deep and steady. And then he went on holding her, until the weight of her head on his arm made the arm go to sleep.

Finally, he had to remove his arm. It did not wake her. He got out of bed quietly and went to stand by the window. They were on the top floor of the hotel, far above the roof lines below, and it was a moonless, star-studded night. But the stars were thinly scattered, their small numbers emphasizing the size of the galaxy, the great, aching, empty spaces that seemed to correspond to the emptiness in his heart.

"Lord God," he whispered, "it is a big thing, your universe, and it is mostly emptiness, and the life you have put here into these places tries so hard to fill the emptiness."

It was the nearest thing to prayer he'd attempted in all of his lifetime. Where he had gone to schools, the Bible had been treated as the one book brought in its entirety from the original world. God, he had been told, had been a provincial god, limited in his power to the one world he had created.

That day he had been given a glimpse into hell, hell as it existed in the mind and memories of an old man who wanted only to be dead. He had seen the far-flung glories of the galaxy, had, from black space outside the reaches of the galaxy, seen with his naked eye the white specks that were other island universes larger and more complex than the one that man had not yet half explored. Big. And the life span of man, at one hundred and twenty years, was but a fractionalized moment.

8

The tenuous and fragile uncertainty of human existence was demonstrated vividly to both Tob and Nema as *Dancer* lifted away from the planet of two suns on flux drive. There was no warning. The malfunction was one of those one-in-a-billion long shots, but machines are made up of mechanical and electronic parts, and if enough nearly perfect machines operate for enough hours, sooner or later one of them is going to hit the odds, that one-in-a-billion long shot that occasionally causes casualties in something as dependable as a spaceship.

At sixty thousand feet the hydrogen-powered flux drive simply quit. *Dancer* was not yet at escape velocity. In the sudden silence there was a lurch as the thrusters lost power and alarms began to clang. *Dancer* continued to rise at a decelerating pace while Tob frantically punched buttons trying, first, to restart the flux thrusters, and then to have the computer make a quick assessment in an effort to locate the problem. He had only seconds before *Dancer*'s upward momentum failed, and there was a moment of motionlessness and then the ship began to fall. The restart procedures, one, two, three, failed. The computer had isolated the problem in flux-drive control. *Dancer* began to fall slowly into a gravity pull that was close enough to Old Earth standard to pull the ship toward a barren plain to the east of the spaceport at an accelerating rate of fall.

Flux drives did not fail. Spaceships carried no escape pods, no parachutes. There was, of course, *Dancer*'s tiny space gig, but not enough seconds before impact for two people to enter, warm the engines, open the port, eject.

Tob had one option left. There were very strict guidelines regarding use of that option, having to do with the inherent peculiarities of the blink generator, the forces of which were still being studied after thousands of years. In open space, the secondary effects of activation of a blink generator dissipated in a spreading bubble from a point of which the ship was the center. If a blink generator was activated near another object, that object, if small enough, would be carried along through the blink. If, however, the nearby object was planetary size, the spreading bubble of force would, first, try to pick up and carry into the blink anything loose, and, secondly, bounce randomly from the planet's surface. Blinking within a planet's atmosphere was, therefore, an offense that, at best, would cost a pilot his license for a long period of time and, at worst, bring imprisonment and/or civil-damage liability.

Tob didn't waste more than five seconds making his decision. He punched in the blink he'd programmed into the computer before takeoff and then *Dancer* was in space, and nothing had followed. He had taken a globe of atmosphere with him, of course, and behind him, just below sixty thousand feet, air rushed into the vacuum with a thunderous roar, and a few people at the spaceport looked up for a moment, but the reflected force of the generator was dissipated without any damage other than a rock slide on a scarp in the arid plain.

"What was all that?" Nema asked, for it had all happened in mere seconds.

Tob was leaning back in the chair, breathing deeply. "I'm afraid I just broke another law," he said.

"So we're all thieves and liars here," Nema said. "We were in danger?"

He explained while he checked to pinpoint the malfunction in the flux-drive control module, opened the hatch, began to test. The small component board that had failed was so simple, so durable, that it was not one of the elements worthy of redundancy. There was no backup system for it. There was a spare, with its carton faded from long storage, and the spare functioned perfectly once Tob had plugged it in.

"Our friends at the shipyard on Golden Haven?" Nema asked, when he told her that that element could not fail.

"Let's take it apart and have a look," he said.

The small circuit board had never been opened.

Its case was molded in place, and there had been no tampering with it. Inside, one printed circuit, with elements so minute that it took full magnification of the ship's optics to see it, had been crystallized.

"I don't think it could possibly have been tampered with," Tob said. "The damage is so minute. It could have been a manufacturing defect, making the conductor just a bit smaller in diameter at this point so that use gradually weakened it to breaking. I don't know for sure, but a cosmic ray, hitting at this exact point, making a bull's-eye on this thread of conducting printing, could have done it."

Perhaps it was because Nema had not been fully aware of the near brush with death, but she wasn't too concerned. Tob, however, found himself brooding about it. If the ship had crashed into that barren plain, the local authorities would have filed a report that, weeks or months or years later, would have become a part of X&A file statistics back on Xanthos. If their personal papers had survived the crash, those who found them would have seen that there were no next of kin to notify, that the addresses were, at least in Tob's case, a forwarding service on an outback planet.

The thought that nobody would have missed him had he died was sobering. And then there was the matter of his split-second decision. At first, as the thing nagged at him, he told himself that he'd been aware of their position relative to the planet's surface, that he'd known that the ship was over an unpopulated, arid area. Yet it nagged at him, for he hadn't given it a thought. He'd been faced with a swift and final decision, a choice between life and death, and he'd chosen life. And yet he'd checked the charts before the landing and before the takeoff. Perhaps his unconscious mind had recorded the fact that the areas around the port were sterile.

It was good to be alive. It was good to let Nema surprise him with her selection for a meal from the ship's dispenser and to eat it on the recreation-room table while watching a new adventure holo.

There would be no more stops between their position and the newly discovered planet where Evan Bender was awaiting, unaware, a contact with two people who were intent on taking his life. Now there seemed to be a sense of urgency, a tenseness that affected both of them. They seemed to want to be together, sometimes in total silence for hours at a time, but each of them unwilling to be alone.

Dancer was functioning perfectly. Her enormous generator, powerful enough to hook onto and lift into subspace and out of it the biggest ship ever built, moved them in multiple blinks through the scattered stars.

Perhaps it was the fact that the malfunction in the thruster control had come very close to adding *Dancer* to the relatively small list of fatal accidents aboard spaceships that brought back to Tob's mind a piece of information that was, at best, a curiosity. While he checked the charts, as the ship edged outward through the Sagitta sector toward the zone called Vulpecula, the name of a planet seemed vaguely familiar, and then, after some thought, he said, "There's somewhat of a space curiosity in orbit around a planet in the next star system. Interested?"

"I'm interested in anything that breaks the monotony," Nema said.

It was only a short detour off their most direct route, and there, cold and graceful in space, was something that might have been the work of a talented sculptor. From either side of a smooth, almost circular asteroid there protruded the prow and bow of a sleek fleet-class cruiser. There was an interesting unity in the object, a sameness of texture and surface. It gleamed in the light of the far sun. A crew of fourteen had died there.

"Why would anyone put it out here?" Nema asked, assuming that the object was man-made.

"It was towed back from deep space, beyond the blink routes," Tob said. "She was an X&A ship, charting new routes. Are you familiar with the process?"

"Not really."

"X&A lays new blink routes at sublight speeds, with very short blinks within the range of their detection instruments. It's a long and tedious process. The captain of that ship was going to speed things up. He made random blinks. he blinked back into normal space in the space occupied by that piece of rock."

Two bodies cannot exist at the same point in time and space. A ship, emerging from wherever it is a ship goes during a blink, is still reassembling. To conform with physical law, and in an effort to occupy identical space, the two objects, an X&A cruiser and a piece of space debris, merged down to the molecular level. Both objects became disassembled, the molecular binding forces confused for a minute moment in time, and now, throughout, that sculpted object there in cold space was a uniform mixture of all the elements that had been present in all parts of the objects. Flesh blended with metal and stone. The result was beautiful, if melancholy.

"That's why Pete Jaynes has been working for decades to try to use the signal that a ship sends ahead of itself as a finder, a detector," Tob said. "So far, at least as far as I know, he hasn't made a breakthrough. That's why we still have ships like *Rimfire* out in the galaxy using their instruments to be sure the space ahead is clear, making a blink of only a few hundred thousand miles, measuring ahead again. That's why, when a new planet is discovered, there's an immediate rush to settle it. Because of the slowness of travel on uncharted routes, we've got a long way to go before we have the galaxy mapped."

"It's oddly beautiful," Nema said, "but it's sad."

"The odds against it happening are astronomical, but it happened."

"Remember that asteroid we caught back off Pandaros? What happens if something like that drifts into a blink route?"

"In full blink a ship isn't affected by something as small as that—will simply pass through it, I suppose. But if a ship comes close to an object of planetary size, it seems that the fields extend into subspace. At best the blinking ship is thrown into an uncomputed corner of space. One X&A ship did that, and it took them five years to chart a route back to traveled space."

Nema shivered. "My planet and my clear stream is sounding better and better to me."

Tob fell silent, blinked *Dancer* away from the long-dead cruiser. His memory went back to the near accident, and he looked quickly at Nema. Funny, he could not imagine her dead. She was so much alive, so beautiful. He could think of himself dead, and although he didn't desire death as Morton Douglas had, he suspected that he wouldn't resist, wouldn't vomit or void his bowels fighting against it.

"Nema, I should take you to your planet and force you to get off the ship," he said; for to think of her dead was a sadness. The pain was not on the order of the pain he still felt when he thought of Tippy, but it was there.

"We've come too far together," she said. "How about a drink of brandy to wash away the morbid mood?"

"You talked me into it," he said, grinning.

Several days later *Dancer* turned outward. The blink beacons she passed were of the latest design. The route was a new one, arrowing toward the big emptiness outside the galaxy. Since Pete and Jan Jaynes' discovery of a life-zone planet so far outside the rim that its star wasn't detectable from the rim, and since *Rimfire* had laid down the blink route circumnavigating the galaxy, both X&A ships and private miners had concentrated on trying to find single, isolated, distant stars outside the galaxy proper. For some reason, such stars seemed to have sizable families of planets, perhaps because, in their isolation, they'd had no competition from other stars in sweeping up the space dust that led to star and planet formation. The planet of their destination was such a star, invisible to the most powerful telescopes from established blink routes.

They were three blinks down the dead-end route, still over five hundred parsecs from destination, when Tob came awake from a deep sleep to Nema's voice.

"Tob, you'd better get in here, quick," she was saying. He leaped from his bed, threw on a robe, and ran onto the bridge, his eyes scanning instruments in search of the problem, for her voice had been filled with urgency.

"Listen," she said, reaching for an attenuator to turn the volumn high on the ship's sublight voice communicator.

The voice came to him over the static of great distances. "Mayday, Mayday, Mayday." A call going back into antiquity, a call universally recognized as distress.

"The ship's monitors just picked it up a half hour ago," she said, "before our last blink. It was too garbled to understand then."

"Mayday, Mayday, Mayday. All ships. Assistance requested, location Blink Beacon VU-779-334-2. All haste."

"You picked it up before the last blink?" Tob asked.

"Yes, dim and not readable."

"Nema, whatever it was is over. That's a light-speed transmission. How long was your last blink?" He was thinking in terms of the parsecs-long blinks they'd been making. Even if the last blink had been relatively short, say two light-years, then two years would have passed, minimum, since the voice had sent out that call for help.

"The route takes a series of jogs in here," Nema said. "We jumped only two hundred thousand miles on the last blink."

Tob grabbed the charts, matched numbers with the last recorded blink beacon. "It looks as if they were just jumping around at random here when they laid the route," he said. "Maybe getting distant readings on something too small to be seen. They're short blinks. VU-334-2 is less than seventy-two hours away at light speed."

"Why would they lay a route with such short jumps?"

"I don't know. Maybe they're planning to come back and straighten it out later. There's always a demand for living room, the way we humans breed. Maybe they started colonization before they could come back and do away with all these short, angled jumps they made while searching." He studied the charts again. "Damn," he said. "It goes on. We have four blinks before we get to VU-334-2, and we're going to travel over one-third more than a straight-line distance."

"It's here?" she asked, putting her finger on the chart. "I see. To get there we have to go here and here and here. If we could jump straight—"

"No deal," Tob said. "That X&A ship might have had some other reason for laying this crooked route. There may be moon-sized dark objects out there. We'll go down the line. Charged?"

"Charging", she said. "I emptied it on the last blink."

There was nothing to do but wait. The generator was slower than usual, for it had to draw on both the radiation and gravitational fields of the distant stars. Tob spent some of the time trying to locate the off-rim star with its life-zone planet ahead in the big darkness, but the ship's instruments were too weak.

"I wonder why there's not a deep-space tug on this route?" he asked, reaching for an X&A Directory, a new copy he'd picked up at their last planetfall. He turned to the Vulpecula sector, followed their route outward, found the newly laid blink route listed and charted, but quickly saw an asterisk. The footnote read: "Vulpecula Outroute Dead End VU-999910 scheduled for tug coverage—" And the date was still some months in the future.

"We can make one blink now," Nema said.

"Might as well wait for full charge," Tob said. "Then we can get there in four blinks and have a bit of charge left."

The Mayday message, obviously recorded, repeated itself every five minutes, sometimes becoming lost in space static. Then the generator was at full charge, and that odd feeling of stress given off by a full generator caused the hair on the back of Tob's neck to stand up. He blinked, programmed, blinked, and blinked again and now the voice was clear and the ship's instruments sang a warning of metallic mass within ten miles of the *Dancer*.

Nema's hands were dancing over the optical controls. "There," she said, as an image appeared on the large screen. Then, "Oh, my God."

The ship was big. She filled the screen on one-to-one magnification. Lights streamed into dark space from her ports.

"A colonizer," Tob said. And then he saw something strange about the ship. The huge vessel was cigar shaped, three hundred yards long, streamlined to be able to use her massive flux thrusters to make planetfall. And there was something weird at her prow.

Nema, too, had noted the oddness. She increased magnification, zoomed in on the ship's prow. "Tob, look," she said.

The colonizer's pointed prow looked as if it had pierced a small merchantman. The space freighter rested across the big ship's bow at about a forty-five-degree angle, but there were no gaping holes, no visible damage. It was as if the two ships had been molded as one.

"Oh, no," Tob said.

"It's just like the cruiser and the asteroid," Nema said.

Tob was toggling the voice communicator. "Colonizer ship at VU-334-2. This is the space yacht *Dancer*. Colonizer at VU-334-2, do you read?"

"Yacht *Dancer*, this is the *Vulpecula Columbus*. What is your passenger capacity? Repeat, what is your passenger capacity."

"They're alive," Tob said, grinning at Nema. Then a huge smile spread over his face. "Do you realize that we're living a tugger's dream?"

"Salvage?" Nema asked.

"She's bigger than *Rimfire*. Not as expensive, but big. And there'll be allowances for human life saved."

"Tob, is this really a time to think of money?"

"We're going to take her in," he said. "We'll be doing the work, why not take what's due for it?"

"And what about the reason we're here?"

"We'll take her to the planet," Tob said. "Great cover. That'll give us a reason for being there. Bender will probably want to meet us and congratulate us. If he's in charge there, he'll be the one who has to inform the owners of the ship that they're going to be hit with a huge salvage bill."

Nema shrugged.

Tob flipped the switch and said, *"Vulpecula Columbus,* am I speaking with the captain?"

"I repeat," the voice said, "what is your capacity for carrying passengers?"

Nema, hearing the voice again after her initial excitement had cooled, went stiff, and brought a hand up to her mouth. She reached over and put her hand on the transmit switch before Tob could say anything else.

"Bender," she whispered. "That's Evan Bender."

"Are you sure?"

"I lived with that voice," she said. "It's Bender."

Tob's face went blank. "Here?"

"Yes," she hissed. "The question is, why?"

"We're still going to have to take that ship in," Tob said. He toggled the switch. "I will speak with the captain of the *Vulpecula Columbus*," he said, "to get his consent to a Lloyd's open contract. If you'll look closely, you'll see that this vessel is a converted Mule II."

"Dancer," Bender said, his voice oddly cold, "the captain and all but one officer of this ship are dead. I am General Evan Bender, military governor of the planet VU-1, as yet unnamed. The nature of the difficulties aboard this ship do not allow salvage rescue. You will lay your vessel alongside, there to take on as many passengers as you can safely carry for a distance of six blinks to VU-1."

"Dancer requires more information regarding conditions aboard *Vulpecula Columbus*, and the exact reasons why rescue salvage cannot be accomplished," Tob said.

"The reason being," Bender said, his voice still cold and calm, "molecular bonding breakdown, the result of direct contact with the small freighter you see at our bow. This molecular breakdown is advancing at the rate of one foot, approximately, every fifteen minutes, the rate accelerating. Should you put a cable on this ship, *Dancer* will become a part of the process."

"How many do you have aboard?" Tob asked.

"Ship's complement of two thousand crew and two thousand colonists," Bender said. "Less those who are dead."

Nema's eyes were wide.

"Chances of other ships?" Tob asked.

"Negative," Bender said. "All communications equipment, except voice communications at the stern, was destroyed on contact."

"Nema," Tob said, "send blink Panic Flashes down both directions. Location, situation." Then, to Bender. "We're sending Panic Flash. In the meantime, we can take no more than one hundred passengers."

"*Dancer*," Bender said, "lay your ship alongside the port lower-quarter stern, twenty-five yards off the hatch marked PS-2. I will come aboard *Dancer* for consultation."

"No," Nema whispered. "Tell him no."

Tob was deep in thought. *They*, men like Bender, were always aware, always looking for an advantage. What an amazing chance it was, to find Bender here, in deep space, on a disabled and threatened ship.

"Affirmative, *Columbus*," he said. He began to ease the ship toward the colonizer. "Weapons," he said to Nema. "The two saffers. Be sure they're fully charged."

"Tob, if you don't kill him the minute he steps aboard, he will kill you."

"Look, Bender may be an opportunist, but I can't see him starting to shoot the minute he comes aboard."

"Tob, you're a thief and a liar. You've stolen a tug and you've falsified papers and misrepresented yourself, and you're still an innocent. There are two thousand people on that ship, and there's one small tug to take them off. Do you think Bender is going to let us blink out of here without him and his men aboard?"

"We'll let only Bender aboard. We'll keep him in the lock while we talk."

"Damn it," she said, "what do you want to talk to him about? Are you going to say, why didn't you find my wife and child and get them off St. Paul?"

He looked at her coldly. Meanwhile, he had positioned *Dancer* and the lock on the colonizer had opened. Four men in space gear floated out of the lock and began to move smoothly toward *Dancer*.

"Bender," Tob said into the communicator, "do you read?"

"I read you, *Dancer*. Open port."

"We're going to allow only one man in the lock, you. Send the others back."

"Negative on that, *Dancer*, the men with me are engineers. They want a close look at the point of joint with that freighter. They have an idea on how to stop the decay."

Tob looked at Nema. She shook her head and gripped her saffer tightly. "You can't trust him."

"Nema, if there's some chance—"

He opened the lock. "All right, Bender," he said, "everyone in the lock."

He readied his saffer. "You stand there," he said. Nema took a position so that both could fire toward the lock without endangering the other. The outer lock door closed and there was a hiss as ship's air filled the chamber.

"We're waiting, Captain," Bender said.

"We'll talk now," Tob said.

There was a moment of silence, then a new voice. "Captain, this is Jack Lansky. I'm chief engineer of the *Columbus*. I saw that you've got weapons, lasers. I think we might be able to use those weapons to stop the decay. I need to use your computer and take a close look forward on the *Columbus*."

"Tell me more," Tob said.

"Captain, there's a reaction on that ship that is unprecedented. In theory, *Columbus* should be a dead ship. She should have merged all molecules with that freighter almost instantly. Apparently, we came out of blink in his space, at a time when his generator was fully charged. He's merged totally with our bow, and the charge in his generator has flowed into the new molecules thus formed. I don't understand how, but instead of an instantaneous merge, the molecular breakdown is proceeding slowly. There's enough charge left in the mass that was the freighter to fuel the change. I'm thinking that we can cut the *Columbus* completely in two forward of a set of airtight bulkheads and separate her from the freighter and stop the molecular decay. Then there'd be enough air left in the surviving section to allow you to blink what's left of the ship to VU-1."

"It would take days to cut through hull and interior members," Tob said. "How long do we have before the decay reaches the point where you propose to cut?"

"I need to use your computer," Lansky said. "I think there's a chance."

Nema shook her head as Tob reached for the switch to open the inner lock door. He pushed the switch and the door hissed up. The bottom of the door had not even disappeared into the recess at the top of the opening when two men flung themselves into the bridge area, saffers blazing, muzzles sweeping back and forth. Nema fired immediately, catching one man in the act of throwing himself to the deck. Tob's saffer sizzled a fraction of a second afterward, the beam of the saffer catching the second man full in the face as he started to turn toward Tob. The third man came in low, and the beam of his weapon flashed and sizzled off a bulkhead, having missed Tob's chest by inches. Both Nema's beam and Tob's played over the moving body as it fell.

In the sudden silence, there was a hiss. Bender had hit the lock controls. The inner door slid down quickly and air exploded outward as the emergency outer lock release was engaged.

Tob ran to the optical controls, swung the sensors over the area between *Dancer* and *Columbus*, saw Bender jetting swiftly toward the open lock on the colonizer.

"The laser, quick," Nema said, leaping to fire control, thrusting the helmet on.

"No, you'll hole *Columbus*," Tob said.

Nema watched angrily as Bender's bulky figure disappeared into the *Columbus'* hatch, and the other door closed.

"Now what?" she asked.

"I don't know. He must be in control of the ship."

"He would be," she said. "Tob, does that colonizer have weapons?"

"I don't think so."

"How many launches?"

"On a colonizer, space is at a premium, as it is on any spaceship. She wouldn't have had more than two launches."

"And two thousand people?"

"It's impossible to provide any ship, except automated merchantmen with a very small crew, with lifeboat space."

"He tried to kill us, you know," she said.

"You were right about him. We won't give him another chance."

"Have you thought that this is St. Paul all over again, in miniature?"

He was moodily silent.

"They know they're going to die," she said. "Bender and his men, and others, will do anything to get off that ship and onto *Dancer*. And if we let them aboard—"

"We can't just do nothing and let them all die. We can save a few."

"Bender will be making the selection of those

who come aboard," she said. "If he gets on board he can't let us live to tell that he tried to kill us, to take over *Dancer*."

Their inconclusive conversation was ended by the hailer. "*Dancer*, this is General Evan Bender. As the legal administrator of this sector of space, I order you to take aboard, immediately, all the people your ship will possibly support."

"We will take aboard, in small groups, one hundred women and children," Tob said.

"That is agreeable, *Dancer*," Bender said. "However, there are less than a dozen children aboard. Most of the colonists are young, many of them unattached."

Tob raised an eyebrow at Nema. That was not the usual makeup of a colonizing group. Young families usually made up the bulk of the people settling a new planet.

"We have only thirty-five suits of space gear," Bender said. "We will begin sending people over. There will be six children among the first group. There will be five men, to ferry the empty space gear back to *Columbus*."

Tob clicked off the communicator. Within minutes the hatch on *Columbus* opened. Suited figures began to pour out. He could not tell children from others, for the suits were large and bulky.

"I don't like it," Nema said.

Tob adjusted the optics. In the van of the group moving slowly and smoothly across the few yards of empty space between the two ships, he saw small, childish faces through the visors. One was a pretty little girl. He guessed her age to be around twelve. Her face showed her fear as it swiveled back and forth, small inside the helmet. But, as the group of thirty-five drew near *Dancer* and he manned the optics, zeroing in on each visor in turn, he saw that all the other suits were occupied by men. Then, hidden behind the first bodies, he saw men carrying tools, torches, clamps for attaching to a ship's hull, weapons in some gloved hands.

Tob flipped the communicator switch and said quickly, "I am speaking to the children in space gear. Hit your jet controls immediately and separate yourself from the main body. Do it now."

One of the children jetted with a thud that reverberated through the hull directly into the side of *Dancer*. Others did nothing. Men jetted forward, and Tob heard the metallic clang of clamps attaching to the hull. He could envision them cutting through *Dancer*'s hull. Explosive decompression would kill him and Nema. There'd be enough reserve air in the emergency tanks to repressure at least the control and drive sections of the ship to give Bender a way to escape death once again. Tob's hands lashed out, activated the flux thrusters. As *Dancer* shot forward men died in the heat and turbulence of the thrusters' exhaust. Tob said, "Brace yourself well." He reversed thrust and they were pressed hard against the deceleration pads. The ship stopped, and the inertial force slung men forward from the hull, sent them spinning out of control into space.

"Hull scan, quickly," Tob ordered. The hull

was clear. A few of the space-suited figures, less than half, were straggling back toward *Columbus* and going into her hatch.

The *Columbus* was silent. Tob moved *Dancer* back to within a hundred yards.

The metal hull showed a smooth, glossy surface where it had been affected by the molecular rearrangement. Tob put an instrument on the area of advance. The deadly decay was moving toward the midsection of *Columbus* at a rate that measured almost a foot of hull per hour. He activated the communicator.

"Bender," he said, "time is running short. I want you to suit up as many women and children as you have gear and send them over. If there are more than two men among them, and if those men try to approach *Dancer's* hull, I'll blast them with lasers."

Bender's voice showed just a hint of stress when he answered. "*Dancer*, as senior officer aboard this ship, I will decide who boards your ship."

"Then no one boards," Tob said.

"I have an offer for you, *Dancer*," Bender said. "Take one hundred people selected by me aboard your ship and I'll see to it that you're paid an amount equal to total salvage of *Columbus*."

Nema took the mike out of Tob's hands. "Evan," she said, "do you recognize my voice?"

"Well, well," Bender said. "I didn't find you, Nema, but you've found me. Listen, it'll be worth your while. I'll pay you whatever you want. You'll have your freedom."

"I have it now," Nema said. "You're going to die, Evan. Do you understand that? You're going to die. You're not getting off that ship."

"Now don't be unreasonable, Nema," Bender began, and while his transmitter was open, there came the sounds of shouts, the sizzling of saffers. Then Bender said, "We just had a little discussion about authority here. My offer is this, Nema. Enough money so that you can live as you like for the rest of your life. Your freedom and legal U.P. citizenship papers."

"Don't you understand, Evan?" Nema asked softly. "You're not in a position to offer or to dictate terms. You're dead."

Bender's voice cracked with anger. "If I don't get off, no one gets off," he said, and there was a click as he turned off his transmitter.

"Damn," Tob said. What could he do? Was he to sit there helplessly and let everyone aboard *Columbus* die? He hoped for a miracle, for a blink stat coming down the route from the rim, for a huge ship to send its signal ahead of itself and appear. Instead, the ship's computer notified him of a blinking light well forward on *Columbus*, within a hundred feet of the moving edge of the molecular decay. For a moment it meant nothing to him, and then he saw that the light was flashing in a pattern of short and long blinks. He had never learned the universal light codes, but it was but the matter of a moment to program a code-reading sequence into the computer.

"Third Officer Borg Daria," the code said, and then repeated. "Acknowledge, yacht *Dancer*."

"*Dancer* acknowledges," Tob typed into the console, and the computer blinked the code from a forward spotlight.

"Request you send man this port." The words came from *Columbus*.

"No," Nema said.

"I can check it out," Tob said. "I'll be sure it's a ship's officer before I go into the port."

"Meet me outside hull in gear," he had the computer send.

"Negative," came the reply. "No gear."

Tob suited up. *Dancer* had only two suits. "I want you to move the ship far enough away so that no one can reach it," he told Nema. "I'll send the word *Pandaros* when I'm ready to come back aboard. If I'm not alone, stay away, and don't open the hatch."

In space, for a moment, he had trouble getting his breath. It always had that effect on him, at first, when he was in gear, out of contact with the solidity of a ship.

Columbus' bulging hull hid him from view from the stern of the ship. The hatch he jetted toward was a small repair hatch, just large enough for one man to enter. It opened as he neared, and then he was inside and the air was hissing in. The inner door opened and he, crouching, covered the soiled, tired-looking man in ship's whites with his saffer.

"I'm Daria," the office said. "Third. Are those pods on your ship lasers?"

"Yes." Tob was still crouched, ready, but Daria was alone. His hair was wet with perspiration and his hands were scratched and torn.

"There's a chance we can save the ship," Daria said. "First we have to get rid of Bender and his commando. They're in control. People have been killed. There was panic when your ship appeared. Bender opened fire, but some of his men were killed. You killed more of them in space. There are only a few left. They're holding the stores areas near the main cargo hatch. I have men ready. We're going to make our way between the double hulls, take them from the air vents and from the rear. When we've eliminated them, we'll use your lasers to cut the ship off forward of the quarter-hull airtight doors."

"A man called Jack Lansky suggested that to me, said he was chief engineer."

"They killed the chief when he tried to restore order after the initial contact with the freighter," Daria said. "Lansky is Bender's unit commander. All the other officers are dead as well. The captain and first died on contact. They were forward in control. Bender killed the fourth."

"How many men do you have?" Tob asked.

"Less than twenty, but we're all armed. We can't tackle them head-on, but we'll have a chance if we take them by surprise."

"All right, let's go," Tob said.

"You should go back to your ship. We'll want you to be ready to begin using your lasers as soon as we have control."

"My . . . partner," Tob said, having trouble finding a word to describe Nema, "is standing by. She can handle the lasers."

"Good, we can use another man," Daria said.

"What about the ship's launches?" Tob asked.

"We had two. They were carried forward. They were destroyed almost immediately."

Daria led the way to an airtight hatch and opened it. Men were waiting in a lounge. Some of them were injured. All were grim and tense, but ready. Daria led the way to a repair access hatch leading to the space between *Columbus'* double hulls. The space was cramped and dark and it took time to crawl over and around the hull supports and the conduits. Tob had shed his space gear in the lounge, and even in his loose one-piece he was sweating.

Daria, halted, cautioned them to be silent. Tob crawled forward to look over Daria's shoulder as Daria opened a hatch and crawled into a work space among large ventilation-system pipes.

Daria directed men into the large vents, led others out of the work area into a narrow corridor. As he rounded a corner he froze and his saffer sizzled. A man in space-commando uniform toppled silently. Daria ran toward a door, flattened himself beside it, and motioned men to come forward. Tob was among them. When the men were in position, Daria nodded, pulled the door open, and dashed through, followed by men who crowded each other to get through the opening, and before Tob could enter there was the sound of wild shouts, the sizzlings and hissings of fire, a hoarse, pained male scream. Then he was in the door, crouched, weapon ready, to see commandos clawing for weapons as the men of *Columbus'* crew fired.

One commando got his weapon out and two crewmen went down before Tob had his weapon aimed and sizzling death at the commando. Then all was quiet.

"That's most of them," Daria said.

"Bender?" Tob asked.

"Not here."

Daria moved swiftly, opening a door on the opposite side of the storeroom, went out on the run. Three other commandos were killed, with the loss of four of the crew, and then Daria was standing beside Tob, panting, in front of a door leading into a living area.

"Colonists' quarters," Daria said. "I have no idea how many commandos will be there." He kicked open the door and Tob followed him into an empty room, then another.

Evan Bender was standing in a sitting area, one of the colonists' lounges, when Daria burst through a door and froze, weapon raised. Tob leaped in, saw that Bender had his arm around the neck of an attractive young woman, whose face showed her terror.

Bender's eyes singled out Tob, by his dress, immediately. "You're *Dancer*," he said.

"I'm Aaron Delton," Tob said. "My wife's name was Tiffany. I called her Tippy. My son was named after me."

Bender pulled the woman closer to him. She tried to scream, but his arm cut off her breath. He had his saffer pointed at Tob. He looked puzzled.

"Those names probably don't mean anything

to you, Bender," Tob said. "They were just two among a billion on St. Paul. But they would have tried to board a ship at your base, because our home was very near. They may have been among those you shot down at the fences, or in the riots."

"Listen," Bender said intensely, "what was it? Delton? I did all I could on St. Paul. No man could have done more. We saved those we could save, just as we have to save those we can save here. You need me, Delton. I can help—"

"As you helped by taking your entire commando off St. Paul? As you helped by trying to kill me and take my ship?"

"Delton, I'm an important man. I have work to do on a new planet. Look, choose those you want on board *Dancer*. Save one space for me."

"No," Tob said.

"Then I'll take this woman with me," Bender said, placing the muzzle of his saffer at the woman's temple. She tried to scream as she gasped for breath, her eyes wild, terrified, pleading.

Tob was in mental pain. The man he blamed for the death of his wife and son was there, in front of his weapon. Time was passing, and each second was precious. There was, according to Daria, a chance of saving almost two thousand lives. He knew none of the people aboard *Columbus*. They were just people, strangers. In his crowded mind were thoughts that the brave men who had fought so well deserved to live, and, rationally, he needed some of them aboard *Dancer*, if the entire colonizer could not be saved, to keep order. And there were two lives before him.

Oddly enough, he no longer hated Bender. Suddenly he realized that he'd been giving in to psychological trauma without logic to blame any one man for Tippy's death. He killed Bender not because he blamed him, or hated him, but because Bender stood in the way of saving many more lives. And his life-and-death decision, made in brief, tense seconds, affected a terrified woman he had never seen before, for she, too, died as he played his saffer over Bender's head.

He was not God. He had made his decision based on time and numbers. Some men had brought out from Old Earth a philosophy that it was better for some to die so that the survivors would have a better life. Tob's decision was not that callous, but it was a decision that cost an innocent woman her life, and then, even as the two bodies fell, he was turning to a shocked Daria.

"Where's the communicator?"

"Next room," Daria said, still looking at the dead woman.

"Get on it. Tell *Dancer* exactly where you want the laser fire. Where are the majority of the colonists?"

"In the cafeterias and lounges."

"Do you have ship's communications?"

"Yes. This is the communications man," Daria said, pointing to a panting young man who had a paralyzed left arm as a result of the fight.

"Let's go," Tob said. "We don't want any panic while we're working. I'll talk to the colonists."

The communications man led the way, flipped switches, handed Tob the mike. "Now hear this," Tob said. "Listen carefully. This ship is, once again, under the control of her crew. We are going to save this ship, and all of those aboard her." He could hear, through an open door, and down long corridors, a faint sound of shouting. "All of you people stay where you are. You will hear the sounds of a laser working. You will not be in danger. We are cutting the forward section of this ship away. Airtight bulkheads are closed, so the mid and stern sections will retain their integrity. Once we have the bow cut away we will blink to VU-1. I repeat. Stay where you are. Do not move around. You will be kept informed. You are going to be safe."

He found Daria in the ship's main communications room, where there was only auxiliary power, and where only the short-range voice communicator was operational. Through a port he saw *Dancer* moving on flux thrusters, took the mike, spoke to Nema to let her know that he was all right, then handed the mike back to Daria, who was consulting a section of the ship's blueprints. *Dancer* was soon in position. Laser beams flashed out. Their sizzling, shuddering impact on *Columbus'* hull was felt as an almost undetectable vibration.

"We have six hours before the rot reaches the area where we're cutting," Daria said. "Thank God she's no armored ship of the line or we'd never cut through in that time."

"Could we cut further back, and give ourselves more time?" Tob asked.

"No. Between the next two sets of airtights there's the mass of the ship's machinery. Where we're cutting now is water storage, air tanks, cargo hulls filled with foodstuff. Easy cutting compared with trying to cut through generators, circulations pumps, all the machinery. Then, too, if we could cut through the machine spaces we'd be without ventilation."

"Six hours," Tob said.

Nema was working well. She alternated lasers to lessen the strain of continuous firing. She moved *Dancer* in a perfect circle around the hull of the colonizer, *Dancer*'s movements directed by the computer and auto pilot, and kept her attention on the lasers. Beams sizzled silently in the vacuum of space, but their impact became louder inside *Columbus* as the outer hull was cut, and the laser beams began working on the inner hull. At three hours water exploded outward from a storage tank, sucked into the emptiness to disappear. Fires started in the cargo holds, and automatic systems worked to put them out until circuits were cut and the fires smoldered in places, were extinguished instantly when explosive decompression occurred after a compartment had been holed by the laser beams.

Four hours. Beams were lancing with unerring aim down through the deep cut that circled *Columbus*. Longitudinal hull supports took a long time to sever. Five hours. The backbone of the ship had been reached by the relentless fires of the lasers.

"By the way," Tob said, with a grin, "as senior officer aboard, Third Officer Daria, do you accept a Lloyd's open?"

"I do, and gladly." Daria grinned.

They were going to make it. *Dancer* pirouetted around the larger hull gracefully, beaming fire, cutting through the trunk lines of ship's function, reaching the strong metal alloys of the ship's central girder. And then the laser beam flashed all the way through into empty space.

"That's it," Nema said excitedly.

"Good job," Tob sent to her. "Now hit the bow section with a flux blast to send it completely away from the ship."

She positioned *Dancer*. Exhaust played over the bow, deflected from the dead merchantman merged at the tip, and the dead part of the ship rolled away into blackness.

"Now hear this," Tob said, on the all ship's circuits. "In about two days we're going to be on VU-1. The contaminated part of this ship has been cut away. We have plenty of air. I suggest that you go to your quarters, if you have quarters left, get some rest. Medical teams work if you can. Ship's crew, especially those involved in food service, please work now. Let's get everyone a good hot meal and then we'll all get some sleep."

"Hey, Tob," Nema called, her voice sounding gay, "everything okay?"

"Okay," he said. "No problems."

"I'd like to have a look," Nema said. "Okay if I hatch with *Columbus* now?"

"Sure thing. Shoot the cable over. Attach it just about amidships. Then lock onto a hatch and join us."

"Cable attached," Nema reported in a couple of minutes. "Coming in."

Large as she was, *Columbus* felt the impact of *Dancer* as Nema brought her hatch to hatch just a bit too hard. The metallic clang reverberated throughout the ship.

"Woops, sorry," Nema said. "No damage."

"They build Mules tough," Tob told Borg Daria.

Tob met Nema in the hatch. She came out of her space gear, donned for safety in case of a leak in the matched lock seals, and gave him a smile that caused him to smile in return.

"Bender?" she asked.

"Dead."

"You?"

He nodded. She came to take his arm, looked into his eyes questioningly. "Are you all right?"

"I'm fine. Let's go meet a few of the colonists, just to reassure them, and then we'll board *Dancer* and blink this multi-million-dollar baby to VU-1."

"I'm with you," she said, clinging to his arm.

Both were shocked to see the condition of the colonists. One large group, in a cafeteria, showed torn clothing, battered faces. A tall, middle-aged man rose from his seat and hurried to shake Tob's hand, then Nema's. Others crowded around.

"What happened to all of you?" Tob asked.

"I think we became less than human for a little while," the tall man said sadly.

"What happened?" Tob insisted.

The man looked away, spoke softly. "It happened when we heard there was a rescue ship alongside. The word was that it was a very small ship, and would be able to take only a few aboard."

"Panic," a woman said. "And I was as bad as any. We fought to get through doors, to get close to the locks. Then the space commandos opened fire and we fought to get away from their weapons."

Nema looked at Tob's serious face. "Tob, come on," she said.

"You're safe now," Tob said.

Nema carried a remote communicator. As they walked down a corridor toward the lock she pressed a check button. *Dancer* was emitting a small but insistent alarm. Tob broke into a run, grabbed a suit. Nema ran ahead, without worrying about suiting up to go through the lock. Tob followed, throwing the suit aside. When he reached the bridge of *Dancer* Nema looked at him with horror. He quickly saw the reason. The computer was recording molecular disintegration aboard *Columbus*. The decay, apparently, had somehow leaped past the point of the cut and was now moving with dismaying speed along *Columbus'* hull. Already, Tob knew, people were dead in the forward areas of *Columbus* nearest the point of severance.

9

"Oh, Tob, no," Nema moaned, "just as they thought they were safe, that they were going to live."

Tob was working at the computer. His first concern was *Dancer*'s safety. The odd currents engendered by the molecular decay that blended all elements into a that smooth, odd substance that was killing *Columbus* were confusing the computer. He got only an estimate of the amount of time he could safely stay in contact with *Columbus'* hull before *Dancer* was fatally affected. To be safe, he cut that time in half. He had less than twenty minutes to get one hundred people aboard *Dancer*.

Who would come? How would the decision be made?

"You stay aboard. Be ready to hit the emergency lock close. Arm the explosives in the lock, and if I tell you to, push the button and blow yourself away from *Columbus*, then stand by to pick up possible survivors in space gear."

"Tob, hurry. Don't take any chances."

Tob quickly set a timer on the chronometer,

and the long second hand began to tick off the time left before almost two thousand people died. "If that alarm goes off and I'm not aboard, blow the locks and get the hell away from here."

He ran back aboard *Columbus*. He had his saffer in his hand. Daria and three members of the crew were waiting at the entrance to the lock, their faces showing concern and question.

"It jumped across," Tob said, his saffer not pointing directly at them, but ready.

Daria groaned.

"I want you and these three men on *Dancer* with me," Tob said. "I'll need you to help me keep order."

"Who—" Daria mouthed, almost silently.

"Women and children?" asked one of the crewmen.

He didn't take time to think. "No," he said quickly. "We have around fifteen minutes. I want each of us to move very calmly, and very quietly. Send the first people you see, in ones and twos, through the lock. The first ones you see."

"Oh, my God," a man said.

"I think I know what you're thinking," Daria said. "If we let the word get out—"

"They'll fight to get aboard," a crewman said.

"Go," Tob whispered urgently. "Quickly."

People began moving toward the lock within four minutes. The timer aboard *Dancer* was ticking. Tob kept track with his remote communicator. Inside *Dancer* Nema met the confused, apprehensive people who were boarding and directed them to pack themselves into the quarters first.

"Ten minutes, Tob," her voice said softly on the communicator.

A mother with a teenage girl hurried past Tob, ran through the lock. A man and wife followed, looking back in fear and question.

Tob had counted fifty people aboard. Six minutes remained before his estimated safety period elapsed. If he was wrong, and *Dancer* had the decay creeping over her hull, all had been in vain. He felt his skin crawl, resisted the urge to dash through the lock, close the hatch, blast away to life and safety.

Four minutes. Seventy people aboard.

A shrill scream came to him from nearby, from the corridor. Borg Daria appeared, trying to drag a protesting woman by the arm.

"No, my husband," the woman screamed, and Daria hit her, hard, and she slumped. Tob leaped forward, dragged her through the lock, saw Nema's concerned face.

"Three minutes," she called out.

Tob ran back to face an advancing mob. The scream, something, had given the alarm. Men clawed, fought, kicked, scratched, as congestion clogged the corridor. Borg Daria and a crewman stood in front of the lock, saffers in hand. Tob fired his saffer at the ceiling, and the beams sizzled and quieted, for a moment, the screaming of the leaders of those trying to fight their way to the lock.

"I can take twenty-six more people," he yelled.

That, he realized immediately, was a mistake. The people crowding the corridor screamed, fought. A woman went down and was trampled as two strong men fought their way out of the arms of those trying to hold them back and rushed toward Tob. He stepped aside and let the two men pass, helpless to do anything else.

"One minute," Nema yelled into his ear. She had come through the lock. "Let's go, Tob. Come on."

Daria and the crewman had their weapons ready, looked at Tob with wild eyes for direction as the struggling mass of people, powered by their own panic, each trying not so much to reach the lock but to hold others back, moved toward the lock.

"Less than a minute, Tob," Nema yelled.

A man broke free and threw himself at Borg Daria, his face wild with hysteria and fear. Daria's saffer fired. The man collapsed onto the metal deck, and the people behind him howled in anger, fear, panic. Other men broke free.

"Daria, through the lock," Tob yelled, and the third officer and the other crewman rushed past him.

And then Aaron Delton, also known as Tob Andrews, faced a decision. Beside him, saffer in hand, stood a beautiful woman. Advancing toward him, giving him only a split second of decision time, were animals intent on survival. And those animals had been, only a few minutes before, subdued, grateful people.

His choice was simple. If he let that mob try

to pack aboard *Dancer*, everyone was dead. He was dead, but that, in that instant, was not the important thing. The thing that tightened his finger on the trigger and sent a deadly beam sweeping the massed humanity in the clogged corridor was an absolute refusal on his part to have Nema dead.

Men fell, women screamed and died. Bodies made a temporary barrier in the corridor and he was moving backward, still firing as others tried to scramble over the bodies, and at his side Nema's saffer was working, too, the two beams sometimes seeming as one. He backed through *Dancer*'s lock, Nema at his side. He hit the emergency-close bottom and the inner hatch slammed down. And then, with another movement of his hand the explosive disconnect charges blew, sending a sharp blow through *Dancer*'s deck into his feet.

In a few steps he was at the controls, and *Dancer* shot away. Behind them, explosive decompression sent bodies, flesh and blood, into space. Behind them a great ship was dying. Her air rushed through the open hatch, emptying her, killing even before the molecular decay, at last, took her, turned all that remained into a dead, smooth-surfaced solidity.

Tob leaned on the control console and wept. Huge, male sobs racked his body, and it was a long time before he realized that Nema's arms were around him, that she was whispering to him, kissing his tear-wet cheeks.

He had never been more alone. The face of the

woman he'd killed with Bender was burned into his consciousness. That face was surrounded by fright masks, openmouthed, screaming, bruised, bleeding, the faces of the mob in the corridor. And then the woman's face was that of Tippy, as clear as if she were real, and the fear and horror on Tippy's face was the same as the woman's he had killed. He was no better than those who had opened fire at civilians on St. Paul. Faced with the choice that had been given both Evan Bender and President Morton Douglas, he had not fled, leaving the decisions to others, but he had delegated it. He had sent Daria and the crewmen to give life to the first people they encountered, a deadly lottery. And, like Bender, he had killed to save a few. To save Nema.

The hurt did not stop with his weeping. He wiped his eyes. Borg Daria was standing nearby, looking a bit embarrassed. Others began to crowd the bridge, emerging from the two crews' quarters.

"Captain," said a white-bearded man, who, before the events aboard the *Vulpecula Columbus*, had been dapper, "I have been elected head of a committee of survivors. It is our request that we be given our fair share of your ship's stores, and that—"

"Your fair share?" Tob asked, his voice hoarse with his weeping. "Your fair share?" He stepped forward, seized the man's lapels, ripped one away. "How did your clothing get torn and soiled? How did you get the scratches and bruises on your face?" He ran his finger down a raw scratch. "That looks very much like the scratch made by a fingernail. What woman did you fight with to try to get onto the ship?"

"Sir," the man said, drawing back. "We have voted, and I did not ask for the honor of being spokesman."

"Your fair share," Tob said. "Your share will be what's left after we feed the women and children. If there's anything left, you will share it. In the meantime, Mr. Spokesman, get your ass off my bridge. Use your committee to distribute survivors among the two quarters and the recreation room. The beds will remain folded into the walls in quarters. No one will come onto this bridge or go into the generator room. Is that understood?"

Behind him, out of the corner of his eye, he saw Borg Daria's weapon rise, level itself at the people crowding onto the bridge. In silence, eyes darting in fear, the people withdrew into the quarters and the recreation room.

"Guard the doors," Tob told Daria and the two crewmen who had managed to get aboard. "I want one look at *Columbus*, and then we'll blink for VU-1."

He took the controls, moved *Dancer* back toward the colonizer, still huge in spite of the loss of her bow portion. Bodies ruptured by the vacuum of space floated, some moving away from the scene of tragedy. *Columbus* was dead. Somehow, once the freighter and the bow had been separated from the main sections, the molecular rearrangement had accelerated. Instruments showed that odd condition that had been measured only once before, the cessation of all molecular expansion or contraction.

There could be no survivors. But suddenly Tob saw movement out in space, turned a scanner toward it, thought for a moment that it was another lifeless corpse adrift, then saw that it was suited. He moved *Dancer* closer, put the space-suited figure directly in front of an optical sensor, and his heart pounded when, in close magnification, he saw, through the visor of the suit, a woman's face. She was crying out, her mouth open and closing. She was alive.

He was putting on his space gear—when Nema came to him. "Tob, we don't know how badly the outer hatch is leaking. It had to be damaged when we blew away from *Columbus.*"

"Get into your gear," he said. "Close off the bridge. Let Daria and the others go in with the colonists and stay there until I get back. If the outer hatch leaks enough to lose all the air on the bridge, you'll have enough to resupply it."

"And you'll be on the outside of the inner hatch. We won't have enough air to open the inner hatch twice."

"I won't leave her out there," Tob said, and she knew that it was useless to try to stop him. She, too, realized the similarity of the *Columbus* disaster with that of St. Paul, and she knew why he'd been weeping.

Both suited, they held their breath as he opened the inner hatch. A wild whistle of air told them that the outer hatch was slightly sprung, and that air was escaping into space, but the loss was minor during the time that Tob took to get into the lock and close the inner door.

Then he was in space, using his suit jets to travel *Dancer*'s length. The woman was still alive, weeping as he closed on her, put his visor against hers, and said, "You're going to be all right." She clutched his suited arms with her gloved hands, and he jetted them gently back to the lock.

The outer lock control would not work. He tried it time and time again. Then he called Nema and she released the hatch from inside. It opened and Tob guided the woman in, began to crank the outer hatch into place manually. Halfway down it jammed. Strain as he might, he could not get it to close, and Nema's attempts to close it with the ship's controls was equally fruitless. With the outer hatch half open, there was no possibility of opening the inner door. Explosive decompression would damage *Dancer*'s bridge beyond repair.

Tob checked his suit. He had enough air for twelve hours. The woman's suit was almost fully charged.

"Nema, are you at full charge?" Tob asked.

"Full charge," she said.

"All right, make blinks for VU-1. We've got twelve hours."

He eased the woman down onto the deck of the lock, put his visor against her, explained to her that all she had to do was press a certain switch with her chin and they could talk by radio.

"Why aren't we going into the ship?" she asked, after pressing the button.

"We can't," he said. "We'll have to ride it out here."

She began weeping.

"We'll be all right. A bit uncomfortable, but safe," he said.

"I have to go to the bathroom," the woman sobbed.

He had to laugh.

"And this is a male suit," the woman cried out.

"Well, I guess you're going to have to put up with wet feet for a few hours," Tob said. "Do whatever you have to do, and then lie back easily. We're going to pretend to be statues. No movement. The more we move the more oxygen we use."

"Are we really going to make it?" the woman asked.

"Honey, I didn't come this far to die in a space suit," Tob said.

"When I heard that the molecular decay had somehow jumped the cut, I knew that we'd all die," the woman said, oddly calm. "I went looking around, looking for a private place, because I didn't want to die with people crying and screaming and looking at me. I found the suit. I had just finished putting it on when I was sucked out an open lock."

"You made it," Tob said. "You did fine."

"I don't want to die in a space suit, either," she said.

"Okay, Just lie back. Think calm thoughts. Breathe regularly but shallowly. The less we move the more we conserve the oxygen we've got."

The hardest part was the time for recharging. Nema got on the hailer to talk to him during that time, telling him they were doing fine, that they had hours yet, that they'd make it.

"Don't take her in too fast when you get there," he told her. "The open lock is going to mess up her aerodynamics. Watch for her to pull toward the lock side when you're in atmosphere."

"I can handle this end," Nema said. "You just breathe as little as possible."

At last the generator was charged, and they were blinking, and there was one more long charge period, but not as long as the last for there was a sun out there now, a lone bright spark in the blackness, the sun of the new planet, and its nearness cut charge time. Tob saw that the woman was either sleeping or had passed out for lack of oxygen. She was, at any rate, at peace. He was feeling very light-headed, and his lungs seemed reluctant to work. It was almost as if he had to tell them, "Breathe in, breathe out, breathe in."

"Tob? Tob, do you hear me?"

The voice came from far away.

"Ummmm," he said dreamily.

"Hang in there, Tob. We're on flux. We're detecting scattered molecules of oxygen, going down. It's a nice planet, Tob, big oceans, nice land masses. There's green there, and I can see large lakes on one continent. And a range of mountains. Snow. I'll bet there are some fine ski runs there. Tob?''

"Yawmnaa," he said, having drunk at least two bottles of champagne all by himself that night he and Tippy celebrated the news that she was pregnant, because she would not drink with a baby forming.

He heard something odd, screaming, and for a terrible moment it was the people massed in the corridor aboard *Columbus*. Then it penetrated. She was going down hot, *Dancer* screaming through thickening atmosphere. Heat. The wild scream of air past the open lock. Nema's voice as the screaming slowed, faded, became no more than a whisper.

"Open your visor. Open your visor. Open your visor."

He couldn't move. Then there was a new sound, a hiss, and a new wailing of wind and hands were turning him and Nema was jerking at his visor and he was taking great gulps of the sweetest, freshest air he'd ever tasted. Before his head could clear she was tearing at the visor of the woman, who lay quiet, and still, and then she had the visor open and was yelling, "Live, damn you, live. He almost died for you."

Dancer was still lowering on flux thrusters. Tob had yanked off his helmet. "Get back to controls," he told Nema.

"Daria's landing her," she said, bending over the woman.

"Get in there," Tob yelled at her, jerking her away, causing her to fall backward onto her rump.

"All right," she yelled, scrambling away on her hands and knees through the open inner hatch.

Tob bent to the woman, opened her mouth, thrust his mouth to hers, and gave her of his breath, thinking, As she said, live, damn you.

The woman's lungs started pumping of their own accord and, seconds later, her eyes fluttered and she tried to rise. He held her down and her eyes were wide and looking into his wildly.

"I told you we'd make it," he said as *Dancer* touched a pad, somewhat roughly. Tob, himself, carried the woman, still in space gear, to the ground, handed her over to medics. The other survivors were being off-loaded. Some of the women were beginning to experience mental trauma as well as the physical trauma they'd undergone. The middle-aged man who had come to Tob on board to announce that he was the spokesman for the uninvited passengers aboard *Dancer*, was one of the last to leave the ship. He would not meet Tob's eye.

Tob had had time to do some thinking as he lay in the open lock, trying to breathe as little as possible. He knew, now, how Morton Douglas had felt. He had not failed as badly as Douglas had failed in deadly crisis, but he had failed.

Whether or not he could have controlled the panic aboard the *Vulpecula Columbus* had he acted differently, was a question that would never be answered. The fact was that he could have put more people on board *Dancer*, more would be alive, if there had not been panic. But it had happened so quickly, so unpredictably, that he'd had only one choice. Was he any different from Morton Douglas?

He knew that he was no Bender. And yet he and Bender had done the same thing. They both had fired upon and killed men, women, and children. That those who died under the beam of his saffer would have died later did not erase the picture of those tortured, screaming, terrified faces. He had looked into man's dark side, and he had seen the mindless animal emerge and claw and fight for survival.

So it was that he felt pity for the middle-aged man who had been involved in the panic aboard *Columbus*. He met the man, put his hand on his shoulder, and said, "Listen, don't let it haunt you."

The man paused, drew back his shoulders, met Tob's eye. "I am satisfied with the way I conducted myself under severe stress, Captain."

And Tob wished that he had that very human ability to lie to himself, wished that he could banish the memories of those terrified, dying faces as the middle-aged man had banished his memories of trying to crawl over the backs of others in order to live.

As he stood there, bemused, Borg Daria came

to him, held out his hand. "You did what you could, Captain. No man could have done more."

And then Dancer was empty. Nema stood, fatigued, her hair mussed, a smudge on her left cheek. Tob called the control tower and got take off clearance, lifted *Dancer*.

"Shouldn't we repair the hatch?" Nema asked as *Dancer* reached the scattered molecules of the upper stratosphere.

"Later," he said. He blinked *Dancer* back to the site of the disaster. Nema, tired as she was, kept the coffee coming and watched without words as Tob positioned *Dancer* atop the dead ship like a cat on an elephant's back, and blinked *Columbus* toward VU-1.

"Salvage?" Nema asked.

"I doubt it. But X&A will need to find out what happened. This will make it easier for them."

The bow section of *Columbus* had drifted off the blink route under the force initially imparted to it by *Dancer*'s thrusters. Soon, after they had slept for ten hours, it, too, was orbiting VU-1. Meanwhile, Nema, refreshed from her sleep, had been dictating an account of *Dancer*'s part in the affair into the recorders.

She had not been finished more than a half hour when the ship's computer informed them of an incoming ship, and, within visual distance, the X&A ship *Rimfire* emerged into normal space. *Dancer* was orbiting the planet near the two parts of *Columbus*. *Rimfire* edged toward them. She was not the newest ship now, but she was still the largest X&A ship, and the most expensive and complete. She had come sooner than Tob had expected, the result of the Panic Flashes he'd had Nema send both ways down the Vulpecula range.

"Yacht *Dancer*, this is X&A *Rimfire*. It looks as if you've been busy."

"Rimfire, Dancer, we felt you'd want the two sections of the ship together and where you could examine them."

"Very good, *Dancer.* We're all very curious. Captain Rainbow extends her congratulations for a job well done and requests that you deliver your report to her in person aboard *Rimfire*."

"Affirmative," Tob said, closed off, looked at Nema. "That's no mere request. They're going to dig deep. Don't volunteer any information about anything other than the *Columbus* affair. Remember that we were coming out to take a look at VU-1 with a view toward settling here."

"I'm a little scared," she said.

"Well," he said, "they can get us for grand theft, that's all."

"Whee," she said, making whoopee circles with one finger. "What's that, life?"

Tob grinned. "I'm hoping they'll be so overwhelmed with our heroics that they won't take too good a look at *Dancer*. Keep your fingers crossed."

He parked *Dancer* near one of *Rimfire*'s ports after explaining that his one hatch was sprung. A repair team jetted across in space gear, and for a few minutes there were sounds of work, then a voice telling them that the outer hatch was straightened, that a new seal had been installed. He popped the outer hatch, checked for leaks, and said, "Thanks very much."

"*Dancer*, be our guest at hatch SP-3, stern port quarter," *Rimfire*'s communicator told them. Within minutes they were walking down a gleaming corridor following the swaying hips of a pert little X&A rating who chattered all the way to a luxurious lounge where a shapely, mature woman in the uniform of an X&A captain stood and held out her hand first to Tob, then to Nema.

"I'm Julie Rainbow," she said. "Welcome aboard."

Tob did the introductions, then said, "Every time I hear your name, Captain Rainbow, I feel that the word famous should precede it."

Julie Rainbow laughed. "Thank you."

"But you're too pretty to be an X&A captain," Nema said.

"This is my day," Julie said. "Thank you, too. I wish I could feel, about what you just said, that it takes one to know one."

Tob looked at Nema. "This lady has blinked *Rimfire* over greater distances, through greater volumns of space, than any ship in history." He looked back at Julie. "I read your account in the X&A journal of your exploration trip to the fringe of the large Magellanic Cloud. It took courage to do unexplored blinks, even out there in intergalactic space. I'm sorry you didn't have time to check out a few systems inside the cloud."

"Another expedition is in the works," she said.

"But please sit down. Coffee? Or something cold?"

"Space juice," Tob said, "what else?" Soon steaming cups of coffee were delivered on a silver tray by a mess girl.

"It was farseeing of you to bring the *Columbus* wreckage here," Julie said. "It will make our job easier. I'm sorry we couldn't get here sooner. It's a terrible tragedy."

"I have our report on tape," Nema said.

"Good, good." Julie looked up and a rating seemed to materialize from nowhere, took the tape, and soon Nema's voice was telling of the *Columbus* disaster. It took one coffee refill to get through it.

Julie sighed. "Well, we'll be working on this one for a while, trying to find out why the two ships didn't merge instantly. I wish Pete Jaynes was here." She brushed back her hair. "Captain, your permission to hook into *Dancer's* computer?"

"Of course," Tob said. He'd been expecting that.

It took only minutes. Then they were seeing the pictures recorded by *Dancer's* optical system, hearing the voices of Tob and Evan Bender, seeing the first attempt by Bender to take over the *Dancer*.

Julie Rainbow shook her head after two hours of listening to audio tapes, those made by *Dancer's* recorders aboard, and these made by a remote unit that Tob had clipped to his clothing as he first boarded *Columbus*. "So your wife and son died on St. Paul?" she asked Tob.

"Yes."

"I don't condone private revenge," Rainbow said. "It's lucky for you that you accomplished that particular purpose under circumstances that won't see you charged with murder."

Tob was silent.

"You knew General Bender, Miss Samira?" Julie asked.

"He owned me," Nema said.

Julie again shook her head. "If only we had enough funds, enough hardware, enough people, we could wipe out that particular barbarism forever. But you, too, seem to have some connection with the St. Paul disaster. I know that Bender was there. I read a report of the investigation of his conduct of the evacuation, and I will say that if I had been on that investigative board, I'd have had more questions for him."

"I was there," Nema said.

"I know," Julie said, "that this whole *Columbus* tragedy must have been terrible for you. It's almost like St. Paul in miniature, isn't it? I'm sorry that I'll have to ask you many more questions. I ask that you understand, and be patient. If you like, you can go planetside. When we want you we'll send down a launch for you."

"We're comfortable on *Dancer*," Nema said, and Tob nodded agreement.

"Good, that will be more convenient and will speed the process. Is there anything you'd like from our stores?"

"No, thank you," Tob said, rising.

"It will take some time to transfer all the

information from your recorders and computer," Julie said. "But the recovery and aid fee from X&A might ease the pain of waiting."

"I'm not familiar with that term," Tob said.

"When a private or commercial vessel aids in the investigation of a space accident, or aids in the recovery of hardware or survivors, payment is made from a special X&A fund. It's based on the numbers of lives saved and the value of the recovered hardware. In this case you saved seventy-six people, and the remains of *Columbus* will be extremely valuable to the effort of finding out what happened. And it's usual for there to be an award from the insurance company involved. That award is a percentage of the fee that would have had to be paid if the survivors had died."

"Well, I wasn't expecting that, either," Tob said.

"You deserve it," Julie said. "Oh, by the way, I'll want to examine your papers. Just a formality."

"Sure," Tob said, thinking, Gulp.

"I'll have someone pick them up, and if you don't have any objections, he'll check out *Dancer* for ship's identification while he's on board." Julie delivered that bombshell with a wide smile.

"No problem," Tob said.

But, on board *Dancer*, the ship still locked with *Rimfire*, he said, "We're in trouble."

"She's such a pretty lady," Nema said.

"That's no lady," Tob said, "that's an X&A

captain. She didn't get a ship like *Rimfire* on her looks."

Nema went to the computer, fiddled with it, turned. "Tob, grand theft doesn't cover it. There are special laws for the theft of a spaceship. Up to thirty years in a work institution."

They had a subdued meal, tried to watch a holo, gave up and went to their separate rooms. Tob's bed was still folded up into the bulkhead. A glove and a scrap of cloth spoke of the presence of the survivors of the *Columbus*. He picked them up, threw them into disposal, and took down his bed, undressed, fell into it, and his eyes popped wide open. He had been tired. He saw Nema, dressed in a shapeless prison dress, doing repetitive, boring hand labor. His eyes ached with the vision. He leaped from the bed and, clad only in his robe, knocked on her door, then opened it.

"Hey, are you asleep?"

"No."

She turned on a soft light, sat up in bed. She wore yellow, and her hair hung loose to her shoulders.

"If they look hard enough," he said, "they're going to discover that this ship belongs to Dunking Deep Space. If they do, I want you to tell them, and I'll back you up, that you had no idea, that you joined me on Golden Haven, not knowing that the ship had been stolen. That won't hold up long, but it might take them awhile to get a check in with Dunking and find out that we worked there together, maybe long enough for you to catch a ship out of here. If it happens, my money, what's left of it, is in the locker under my bed. Take it."

"You'd do that for me?" Nema asked. "Why?"

"Why not? No need for both of us going to prison."

"Maybe they won't check that closely."

"Maybe."

He stood there uncertainly.

"Are you going to stand there dressed in that disreputable robe all night?" she asked, smiling.

"I don't know. Can't sleep."

"Come here," she said, patting the bed beside her. "I'd like for you to hold me, just for a little while."

He lay down beside her. She threw the light covering over him, put her arms around him. Her nightwear was filmy. The warmth of her came to him.

"I won't let them take you away from me," she whispered fiercely. She laughed. "You're my security blanket."

"Nice to know I'm valued," he said, chuckling in spite of himself.

"You're my friend, Tob. The only friend I ever had. I can't imagine being without you."

Things were happening to him. Images flashed into his mind, burned, disappeared. The scenes on St. Paul, first, and it was as if, somehow, he was erasing them instead of reviewing them. Her breath on his neck was warm and sweet. He pushed her away, struggled out of his robe, gathered her into his arms.

"Better," she whispered, then she caught her breath as he removed her nightwear. "What are you doing?" she asked archly.

"You don't have anything to do until morning, do you?" he asked.

"Just sleep a little," she whispered, pressing close.

"We can sleep when we're dead," he said.

"What *are* you doing?" she whispered, as he began to caress her.

"My friend, Nema," he said into her ear, "since neither of us has anything pressing to do for the next few hours, I thought now would be as good a time as any to lay a ghost."

She laughed her deep, throaty laugh. "Thank you, sir, but I feel very much alive." Then her eyes went wide and she clung to him.

"Maybe more than one ghost," he said, "so be patient. It may take awhile."

It did. He held her, whispered to her, caressed her, kissed her, for a long, long time. And then that wasn't enough. "Don't fake it," he told her in a furious, desperate whisper, stopping what he was doing and going back to soft kisses, lingering touches, whispering praises of her.

"I said not to fake it," he told her much later, and then, once more, started all over.

It took a long time. When it happened, there were no sharp cries, no heavings and pantings, no theatrics as in some gaudy holo love scene. Time and again she had said, "It's no use. It's no use." And time and again, although he burned, he was patient, and tender, and loving, and then there was a new tension in her that could not be faked, a wide-eyed surprise that made him grin, and kiss her, and continue until, with a quick little soft murmur of total happiness she gave herself to him and knew the thing she'd never known.

She wept softly, heartbroken. "Why?" she whispered. "Why now? It isn't fair. It just isn't fair. To find *you* like that, and then to think that they might take you away from me."

He held her, kissed her, soothed her. She jerked away and sat up. "Is that love, Tob?"

"Maybe. How do you feel about it?"

"I know that I want to spend the rest of my hundred and twenty years with you."

"Maybe that's love."

"No ghosts?"

"I'll always remember Tippy," he said.

"I'd want you to, but I'll forget."

"If you want to."

They were awake when the ship's clocks said it was morning. Men from *Rimfire* came aboard, took their papers, began to check the registration numbers of *Dancer*. The men went away. A call from *Rimfire* asked quite courteously that they meet Captain Rainbow in the lounge.

They were escorted by a young man who did not chat amiably the way the girl who had first shown them to the lounge had. Julie Rainbow sat alone in the room, did not rise when they entered. She motioned them into chairs.

"Your papers are very good," Julie said. "Yours

a bit better than Miss Samira's, Captain Andrews. Some of the best forgeries I've ever seen."

"The man who sold them to me said they'd fool anyone, even X&A," Tob said.

"Almost," Julie said, with a disarming smile. "We've gone over the events of your part of the *Columbus* disaster. Under ordinary circumstances I'd put both of you in for the civilian space medal."

Tob looked at Nema. He wanted to store as much of her as possible in his mind. He waited for the other shoe to fall, for Rainbow to say that she knew *Dancer* to be a stolen ship.

"You told Evan Bender, aboard *Columbus*, that you are Aaron Delton," Julie said. "We burned up a lot of credits in blinkstat time overnight to find out that Aaron Delton has nothing against him on the record, that he went down to the surface of St. Paul after the disaster and was presumed to have been killed. Why would you then work and travel with faked papers?"

"I took a launch from the *Hendron Messenger*," Tob said.

"The theft of a space vehicle is a serious matter," Julie said. "But the *Hendron Messenger*'s recorders showed that you confronted the ship's captain when he refused to obey an X&A Panic Flash. You then took the *Messenger* to St. Paul, where she performed valuable service in taking survivors to a safe planet."

"Some good, some bad," Tob said, not knowing what else to say.

"And you risked your life, both of you, in

rescuing people from the *Columbus*. Going out a damaged lock, not knowing whether or not you'd be able to return to the ship ... That was quite a thing, Captain."

"I'd seen enough people die," he said.

"And in all of your time aboard *Columbus* you acted in a seasoned, legal manner, carrying a remote-to-record voice into the *Dancer's* records. That alone will make our investigation easier. And the sound recordings will give the professors who study human nature something to talk and argue about for years. You conducted yourself well. You saved seventy-six lives. What am I to do with you?" She shook her head. "False papers."

Tob was beginning to hope. She had not mentioned the theft of a Mule II tug.

"I should, at least, take your false papers and send you to the nearest X&A post for questioning," Julie said.

Well, there it went. They'd find out the truth about *Dancer* sooner or later.

"On the other hand, they are very good false papers, and it would take the advanced equipment aboard *Rimfire*, or study in the main lab on Xanthos, to see that they're false. Do you suppose that there could have been some malfunction in our equipment? We've been in space for a long time, and the instruments for examining papers and documents are seldom used."

Nema looked at Tob with a smile. "We lost thrust not long ago because a component in the thruster control went bad. Tob said that component never failed, but it did."

"Equipment does malfunction," Julie said. "You *don't* plan to use those particular papers to go into any commercial activity involving your nice little yacht, do you?"

"No," Tob said quickly.

"Converted second-generation Mule, isn't she?" Julie asked.

"That's right," Tob said, going cold inside again.

"Pete and Jan Jaynes were on a Mule when they pulled *Rimfire* back from subspace when we were stuck," Julie said. "Versatile ships. I'd like very much to see what you've done to convert her."

"Our pleasure," Nema said. "Why don't you have dinner with us tonight?"

"Thank you," Julie said. "We should be finished with you by then." She rose, pulled a paper from her pocket. "While we were burning up the routes with blinkstats last night I got authorization for this."

This was a check. Tob looked at it, did a double take. It was for universal credits, was in ten figures, but it was the very first two figures that made him blink.

"The insurance reward money will be delivered to you later," Julie said. "One hundred thousand per person."

"Captain," Tob said, "you've just made me decide to serve you our last Pandaros steaks tonight."

"Ummm," Julie said. She stood watching as Tob and Nema left, Nema's hand going up to clasp Tob's arm. Her first officer, a handsome man, stepped into the room.

The first officer smiled at her, shook his head. "I hope I'm never asked to explain why you're having dinner aboard a stolen space vehicle," he said.

"You won't, Brad," Julie said, "because the records have been erased and we're going to forget that you found the original serial numbers by checking metal stress under the altered numbers." She smiled. "Aren't we?"

"I'm willing to forget anything that will keep us from heading back toward the Cloud," the first officer said.

"Good, good. Let's wrap up our part of this quickly. The lab boys will be here soon to study *Columbus*. Meanwhile, I have a dinner date."

Julie Rainbow was out of uniform when she boarded *Dancer*. She was nothing short of spectacular in an evening dress, and for a few moments Tob let his eyes feast on two beautiful woman, before, without any problem, his attentions were directed mainly toward Nema, who glowed in one of the creations she'd purchased long ago and far away in a fashionable women's shop with Tob looking on and voicing his opinions about her choices. The meal was spectacular, too. Well aged Pandaros steaks, after the synthesized meats that were X&A shipboard fare, made Julie smile, gave her a sense of well-being. And the looks passed between Tob and Nema caused her to be nostalgic. When she had been younger, she'd looked at her captain, Dean Richards, in much the same way.

"So," she said, over a glass of fine brandy, "now that you're finished with all our nosy questions, what will you do with all that lovely money?"

"Well," Tob said, "we owe some money on *Dancer*."

Nema shot him a questioning look.

"And then we're going to look for a U.P. planet where we can buy some land with a clear, cool stream and build a house with a deck out over the stream so that when we wake up in the morning we just have to walk out, fall in, and never have to take a shower."

"I'd be careful of legalities in paying off this ship," Julie said, and there was a tone in her voice that made Tob look at her quickly. "But I envy you the clear, cool stream. By the way, you might want to take a look at VU-1. You're here. It's a U.P. protectorate. I made a strong recommendation by blink stat last night that we stop using private contractors, such as General Bender. When I told them about his actions on the *Columbus*, and what you'd told me about what he did on St. Paul, the director agreed. There'll be a retired X&A admiral as governor of VU-1 until they have elections. It's a great planet. I don't think you'll have any trouble finding your spot."

"Good idea," Tob said. "We'll have a look."

They stood by the airlock, two beautiful women

and a very happy man. Julie shook their hands, smiled. "By the way, Tob, I was reading a very interesting study last night. It had to do with altering serial numbers stamped into metal."

She looked into his eyes, her smile not fading.

"X&A doesn't want it to get out, but some clever man has discovered that there's a way to do away with the internal metal stress that can be detected when a serial number is stamped."

"Fascinating," Tob said, wondering. "What now?"

"Yes, it's easy to file away a serial number and stamp a new one, but the internal stress leaves a permanent record of the original number, unless someone takes a molecular bonding welder at low heat and cooks and rearranges the affected molecules. Isn't that interesting?"

"Damned fascinating," Tob said as Julie swept regally through the lock and the door of *Rimfire's* lock opened.

"I think giving you a medal would be going too far, don't you?" Julie asked, as a parting shot, smiling over her shoulder.

10

From VU-1, still officially unnamed, three objects were visible in the night sky, not always at one time. First and most spectacular, the distant spiral form of the galaxy, tilted slightly, filled the northern skies. Then there was a moon that had standard phases. And, visible from the northern hemisphere just above the southern horizon was the Great Magellanic Cloud.

In the year since Captain Julie Rainbow had dined with Nema and Tob aboard *Dancer*, a lot had happened. Far away, on the opposite side of the galaxy, a well-bonded delivery firm had landed a brand-new second-generation Mule tug on Pandaros, the papers made out to Dunking Deep Space Ltd. The delivery had not been announced in advance by the Dunking home office for good reason. Dunking had not ordered the tug. They had long since written off The *Emily X. Dunking* as being lost in space. Actually, the new tug made life more difficult for John Madison, Dunking's resident manager, but his wife smiled, took his hand, and said, "They're alive, John, isn't that nice?"

Captain Julie Rainbow, commanding *Rimfire*, was at the edge of the Great Magellanic Cloud, starting the laying of blink routes along the rim. In two months of exploration *Rimfire* had discovered two water planets, blue and beautiful.

In the foothills of a great, snowcapped mountain range on the northern continent on VU-I, Mr. and Mrs. Tob Andrews, citizens of the U.P., had watched their house go up bit by bit. Mrs. Andrews, a tall, lithe, dark, and beautiful woman, made several merchants in the growing city nearby happy with her orders for furniture and decor. And a small church in a little agricultural village near the Andrews home was growing pleasingly, with Mr. and Mrs. Tob Andrews as members.

"A church, Tob?" Nema had asked, when Tob told her where they were to be married.

They'd been standing on the site of their future home at the time. There was no moon. The galaxy was the light in the sky, and it showed them its perfect, spectacular spiral arms beautifully in the clear, cloudless night.

"Can that be an accident?" Tob asked. "And some of those stars we see are other galaxies. Think of the life that's there, in just that one. Man. The animals on planets like Pandaros. Think of the human brain. Accident?"

It was an impressive service, their wedding. The music was said to be ancient. The minister spoke words of beauty, of a time when the morning stars sang on Old Earth, and as time passed, and they heard other words, and read them for themselves, the last of their ghosts faded.

"We've seen the dark side, the evil," Tob told her. "Let's see if we can find the good, the light. It's a belief that has lasted for thousands and thousands of years. Let's give it a chance."

"Are we going to become mystics?" Nema asked.

Tob laughed. "Got anything else to do?"

A year later, both had forgotten Nema's cynical remark.

About the Author

ZACH HUGHES is the pen name of Hugh Zachary, who lives with his wife, Elizabeth, between salt marshes and the sea on a North Carolina island. Although science fiction is Hugh's first love, he is prolific in other writing fields as well, often in collaboration with Elizabeth.

Hugh Zachary has worked in radio and TV broadcasting and as a newspaper feature writer. He has also been a carpenter, run a charter fishing boat, done commercial fishing, and served as a mate on an anchor-handling tugboat in the North Sea oil fields.

Hughes' science fiction novels, *Killbird*, *Gold Star*, and *The Dark Side* are available in Signet editions.